NEVER LET
a STRANGER
in YOUR HOUSE

Also by Margaret Logan

Fiction:

The End of an Altruist

C.A.T. Caper

A Killing in Venture Capital

Deathampton Summer

Nonfiction:

Happy Endings

Never Let a Stranger in Your House

Margaret Logan

St. Martin's Press ⋈ New York

Design by Basha Zapatka

Library of Congress Cataloging-in-Publication Data

Logan, Margaret.
    Never let a stranger in your house / Margaret Logan.
        p.   cm.
    "A Thomas Dunne book."
    ISBN 0-312-13130-5
    I. Title.
    PS3562.O4478N48   1995
    813'.54—dc20   95-5230
                                                        CIP

First Edition: May 1995
10 9 8 7 6 5 4 3 2 1

For Elsa, Rockwell, and Mary Lane Townsend

Never Let a Stranger in Your House

1

Olivia Chapman opened her front door and stepped into postcard Boston. The morning sun was brilliant, the wind scouring up Joy Street had an autumnal edge. She tightened the scarf around her neck and faced into it, heading downhill to Mikey's, the corner store.

The leaves of the Bradford pears on Pinckney Street had started to turn. She'd seen them planted, what, a dozen years ago? Spindly then, they'd grown strong and tall, a double file that traced the street's long, graceful run down to the river.

Spring was their dramatic season, tourists' cameras snapping away at the foamy explosion of bloom. But to Olivia's eye, the fall display, rosy purple burnished with gold, was more beautiful. Especially on days like this, the clear light delineating every age-mellowed brick and precious detail of the historic houses.

The last time the leaves had turned, Olivia's husband Philip had been alive—as alive as a man can be entering a second year of coma. This anniversary she would keep to herself. Mention it, or note any other difference between then (Philip alive) and now (Philip dead), and out the word would go. Kristen Jacobs, for instance, the neighbor across the street she'd just greeted—

kindhearted Kristen would broadcast up and down Joy Street that Olivia Chapman was brooding. Being morbid. "You'd think it was a mercy," she'd say, her eyebrows knitted with concern, "him finally passing on after so much time. A release. But I guess you never know, do you?"

Olivia did feel released. In one sense, Philip had died the instant that drunk teenager's pickup smashed into his motorcycle. Waiting for the rest, managing hope (miracles can happen) had been very hard. The shocker was that release, when it finally came, had carried no immunity from grief and desolation.

He'd died in June. A few weeks after the funeral, Dee Quintero, a close friend since college days and the second-floor tenant of her town house, had found her in her street-level office. "Up for a walk?" he'd asked. "It's glorious out, and I've got errands."

"Can't," she said. "The kids might call."

Her teenaged sons, Abbott and Ryland, had returned to their summer jobs in Alaska and New Hampshire. She hadn't clutched them to her bosom, tried to draw sustenance from their freshness and energy. Good mothers don't clutch and cling. They kiss their children lightly and send them on their way.

"We won't be long. They can leave a message on the machine."

"Yeah, but look at all this *stuff*." Olivia gave her desk an agitated wave.

"What stuff? I've never seen your desk so neat."

They argued back and forth until Dee touched her hand. "Olivia? Want to listen to yourself?"

Stopped short, she heard the reverberation of her shrill, panicky excuses. "It's okay," said Dee, pure kindness. "No giant steps. Once around the block and we're home."

"Someone will *talk* to me." She blinked, astonished. Until this blurted admission, she hadn't known that she was afraid, scared stiff. She thought she'd simply been lying low, keeping

2

quiet, healing. Her clients—only a few in summer anyway, slack season for interior decorating—had said, Don't worry, take all the time you need.

"Just to the Common," Dee coaxed. "We run into someone and you don't want to talk, I'll handle it."

That first excursion had left Olivia soaked with sweat, her heart pounding. The street had seemed an assemblage of painted flats. The voices of the people they'd met had sounded muffled, as if coming from behind masks.

The next morning she and Dee had walked out again. And the next. Weeks later, she attempted a solo and survived with manageable symptoms. Now her phobias were history. To keep them that way, she began every day with this walk to Mikey's. Rain or shine. It was a maintenance task, like muscle stretches or flossing.

A sudden gust snatched the door from her control. "Sorry," she said to Mikey as the wrenched hinges complained.

"No problem. Sucker busts loose, I got insurance. Do it right this time."

"Chicago's supposed to be the Windy City," one of Mikey's regulars offered, "except I read they measured both places and Boston's much worse."

Another man gave a derisive laugh. "You should've read to the end of that piece. Chicago got named 'windy' account of people were always bragging."

The first man didn't get it.

"Windbags," explicated the third member of this morning's group.

Mikey's was a relic of the old, ungentrified, north slope, the half of Beacon Hill that sends no images to the popular imagination. (The south slope has the famous streets, architecturally splendid and shaded by ancient elms.) North-slope houses like Olivia's might be historical prizes, but around the corner were grim tenements and grimmer institutional buildings. In the late 1970s, when south-slope real estate moved from pricey to totally outrageous, gentrification of the north slope became inevitable. Condominium associations sprouted like mung beans; young families poured everything they could beg or borrow into the renovation of near-derelict properties. A new mayor, partial to the downtrodden in ways beyond the imagination of his imperial predecessor, checked this process somewhat. A surplus school could become elderly, but not yuppie, housing. And developers could more easily pass a camel through a needle's eye than convert any more rooming houses to condos or market-level rentals.

Most of the men who hung out in Mikey's lived in the rooming houses that had escaped conversion. Some were on Social Security. Others, for emotional reasons, were unemployable except as strong backs, casual labor waiting for someone to mention that a cellar needed clearing or a kitchen gutting. You wanted a fridge humped upstairs on the cheap, your best bet was Mikey's, aka the Hillside Spa.

Why "Spa"? The original shop had been larger, with a soda fountain. Such places, in New England, were often called spas; today you can still hear "tonic" for carbonated drinks of all sorts. Mikey's nod to the past was an elbow-high shelf for the regulars' ashtrays and Styrofoam coffee cups. There was no seating. No room for it, and no desire on Mikey's part to draw bureaucratic attention to the Spa's unlicensed and profitable coffee urn. As it was, the new people, the condo people, were constantly screaming about loitering and litter. It burned Mikey up. So did their proclamations of the superiority of urban diversity to the boring old suburbs. "Just don't let any diversity sit on their front stoops," he'd growl. "Then it's whoa, Nellie."

Plus, the piss issue. "The streets can run with piss from the condo dogs, but any diversity hopes to take a leak? The cops get called before the poor bastard finishes unzipping himself."

Olivia picked up her paper, laid her money on the counter.

Never a smiler, Mikey always thanked, even for thirty cents. "No milk today?"

"Appreciate the reminder, but I'm set."

"You hear about the Lyman house?"

The men at the counter fell silent. Mikey's rumors were famous, and so was the Lyman house. Decayed grandeur in the very heart of the south slope, it had stood empty for months, exciting endless worried speculation about its future.

Looking Mikey in the eye, Olivia played her part. "Has it been sold?"

"Nope. It's gonna be for the homeless. What they call SROs." Mikey's laugh was merry. "A joke, I thought it was. Standing room only, like, on your feet, you bum, get offa my front stoop. Turns out it means 'single room occupancy.' A flophouse, basically, but high-class."

Olivia, still playing: "And is Chestnut Street happy about this?"

Mikey rolled his eyes. "I guess the lawyers're happy, assuming they hired local. Hey. You're a decorator, right? Maybe there's work in it for you."

Not a peep from the regulars. Olivia felt them watching. "We'll see," she said, making for the door.

After the cigarette fug, the air outside shocked with its purity. Olivia liked the wind nudging her homeward.

It was odd that Mikey had salted today's con with a personal twist, dragged in decorating, her bread and butter. Normally, the fun of the game was restricted to what happened when the rumor came back to the Spa on the lips of some gullible newcomer. The regulars had to stay deadpan as Mikey reacted. "Yeah? This on the level? Mind telling me where you heard it?" Only when the mark was safely out the door could everyone crack up, laugh to split a gut.

Having been snookered herself once, Olivia knew exactly how it worked.

This morning's con, a wicked petard that hoisted the richest

5

street on Beacon Hill, should travel far and fast. For years Lyman House had sheltered the small staff and genteel functioning of the Boston Center for World Harmony; Henry Lyman, the non-resident owner, had become an ardent pacifist in his eighties. Last spring he had died at the age of ninety-three, passing the house on to his grandson Bowditch, called Boy. According to the Beacon Hill grapevine, Boy had been loitering in Bangkok when he learned of his inheritance. Instantly he got on the phone to terminate the harmonists' lease. By summer's end, they were gone, and he was back in Boston.

What gave Mikey's joke a special twist was that the south slope's limousine liberals had stood foursquare behind so many other Beacon Hill conversions. It was only right, they'd proclaim, only fair and decent, that a surplus public school on the north slope be turned into low-income housing. Or that Beacon Hill's sole synagogue, also on the north slope and long-emptied by population shifts, should become a residence for "the developmentally challenged." The tone of these activists was earnest, convinced, impatient. "Integrating special-needs populations with the wider community is no big deal," they'd say. "Denmark's done it for years. No NIMBY nonsense there."

The north slope, even those souls who wandered the streets conversing chiefly with themselves, soon noticed that there were no pro bono conversions, proposed or accomplished, on the south slope. But the north's efforts to put the NIMBY shoe on the south's foot were vigorously protested. "The north slope," huffed the southerners, "is simply where these schools and other big old arks happen to be situated."

With the singular exception of that big old Lyman ark.

A woman approached from the top of the hill, her outfit claiming Olivia's attention. A short, swingy coat in this fall's big color, a dusty olive green, tights and elf boots in the same shade showing off a pair of good legs. The woman's short hair

6

was artfully curled and streaked. Huge sunglasses kept half her face a secret.

"Olivia? Don't you recognize me?"

"Lori? My God."

Lori Lutz's laugh admitted the full extent of her transformation. Usually she mooched around in sweatpants or fringed, shawled, draggle-hemmed rigs evocative of the sixties, her long hair in a signature braid halfway down her back.

She and her husband, Rob Mallory, were both writers in their mid-thirties. They'd rented an apartment a few doors from Olivia until last year, when they bought a house on Mount Vernon. Beacon Hill's obsession with real estate ensured that everyone knew what they had paid: eight hundred thousand. Few questioned the desirability of a change from north to south slope, but questions about why this couple wanted a house so large remained unsatisfied. Almost certainly they did not intend to fill it with children; Rob had celebrated his twenty-first birthday with a vasectomy. "If most men did the same," he'd inform you at the drop of a hat, "the world would be a better place."

Olivia told Lori she looked terrific. "Great coat. Great color."

"Really? It's for this book tour I'm doing. Today's my test run. It's really a suit. See?"

She flipped open the coat, posing awkwardly. Her short skirt showed another two inches of not-bad thigh. At the neck of her creamy silk blouse was an adroitly tied scarf, jungle greens spiced with gold and red.

"Fabulous," said Olivia. "I love it. I want it."

Lori's smile stayed tentative. "Thanks, Olivia. I did this yesterday, the whole shebang. I woke up feeling awful—I really dread these tours—and dragged myself over to Neiman-Marcus. They have this amazing woman there. Monica. A true believer, you know? She hasn't even had her coffee yet, but the minute I say 'book tour,' she's all mine. Heart and soul. After we do the clothes—this red in my scarf? Pimento, Monica calls it? I've got pimento stockings and boots, too, in case I feel like a change. Anyway, once we finish the clothes, Monica sends me over to this chichi salon on Newbury Street so her buddy Renee can fix the rest of me.

"And guess what? All these chichi women who're having their hair done? Their nails and all? They keep yelling out how much they love my books. Isn't that amazing? So by the time Renee tucks me into her private sanctum, I'm Silly Putty. Whatever she's selling, I'll buy. She personally does the haircut and supervises the rest. I got shampooed, highlighted, facialed, massaged, tweezed, manicured, pedicured, leg-waxed, and made up. I got a bunch of cosmetics in a little case and a lesson on how to use them. What do you think of my"—a self-conscious laugh—"maquillage? Did I pronounce that right?"

"You did and it's fine. Very natural-looking." In truth she had overdone the foundation, but practice ought to fix that.

Lori's ingenuous astonishment that her reading public was large enough to include the pamperati fit with what Olivia had observed before. She spoke of her writing only when pushed, and then as if it were some sort of hobby, not work that had enabled the purchase of an expensive house. "Basically I concoct a bunch of people, give them a bunch of problems, and write up what happens," she'd say. *Sweet Harmony*, her latest, was stacked in the window of every bookstore. Her commercial success drove Dee, in every respect the opposite sort of writer, bananas. "Dreiser was right," he'd fume. "What the American public craves is tragedy with a happy ending."

"The thing is," Lori now scrupled, "it's not *me*. You know? I catch myself in a mirror and I'm like, hey, who's that?"

"*I'd* be like, hey, there's one fine-looking woman."

"That's so nice to hear. I really appreciate the support."

There was something strange about the way she was talking,

a touch of Boston Brahmin lockjaw with different vowels. (Lori was from the coalfields of Pennsylvania.) Wasn't one side of her face a little puffy? Tooth problems? Lousy break, teeth acting up on the eve of a public-appearance tour. But if Lori didn't mention it, Olivia wouldn't, either.

They chatted a bit about the cities she'd be visiting. Then: "So you really think I'll be okay? This skirt's not too short?"

"Before I saw it was you, I had three thoughts. The first was along the lines of, Wait, am I in New York? Paris? Next, Too bad everyone in short skirts doesn't have legs like that. Then the bedrock: How, in the face of this elegance, dare I be such a slob?"

Lori laughed, her mouth protectively lopsided. "Some slob. When Renee asked me whose hair I liked, I told her about yours. It's hard to tell in this wind, but see?" She turned around to show Olivia the layered and tapered back.

"I'm flattered. Rob likes it?"

"Oh, sure. You know Rob."

As a matter of fact, Olivia didn't. She seldom saw Rob on the street, and the few times they'd met at neighborhood gatherings he had been either aloofly silent or carrying on in his obnoxious vasectomies-for-all mode. "Will Rob," she asked, "be with you?"

Above the sunglasses, a startled frown. "What do you mean?"

"On your book tour. Doesn't he sometimes come along?"

"Oh. Not this time, no. But what about you, Olivia? How are you doing? How are the boys?"

"We're all fine. Ryland broke up with his umpteenth girl, but there are hints that Abbott, at long last, has found his first. Why did I put it that way? Let's start over. We're fine. Abbott may be in love, but Ry's a free man."

"Oh, Olivia. You don't really mean that. You still believe in love, don't you? *I* do."

Love Conquers All, Dee had scoffed, was the fundamental principle of the Lutz happy ending. "Love's grand," Olivia said, giving it a grin.

"Just before? When you hadn't recognized me yet? You had this nice smile, lit up your whole face. I was so happy for you."

One bad thing about being a widow was the freedom people felt to say this sort of thing right to your face. "I was just in the Spa. Mikey's floating a good one today. The Lyman house is going to be low-income housing."

Lori's expression changed dramatically. "It's no rumor."

"You're kidding."

Stiffly: "You want me to be kidding?"

"Not at all. But the Chestnut Street I know likes its good works kept at a safe remove."

"You can say that again. We're expecting a fight."

"We?"

"Boy asked me to be on his board of directors. It's really neat, Olivia, the way the whole thing came together. He was staying in this guest house in Thailand? And some other Westerner left this paperback behind? Boy was so famished for reading material, he dived right in and went pretty much nonstop to the end. Now here comes the spooky part. He's just closed the covers of the book, right? There's a knock on the door, a telegram. 'Your grandfather has died and left you the house on Chestnut Street, love, Mother.' Okay, what was the title of the book?"

"Let me think. Houses, right? *Rebecca*?"

"Guess again."

"*Howards End*?"

"Oh God, I'm embarrassed. You probably never even heard of it. *3 Hots & a Cot*?"

Of course. Lori's second book was set in a shelter for the homeless. "I've not only heard of it," said Olivia, "I read it with pleasure." A lie, meant generously. Generosity had sent her to the book in the first place. "A neighbor spends her life writing," she'd said to disdainful Dee, "I can at least take a look." Unfortunately Dee had been right: not her kind of book.

She retreated to safer ground. "How wonderful for you, knowing your work had such an impact."

Lori's lopsided smile turned wry. "Especially when *3 Hots* didn't make back the advance. Oh, well. If you and Boy were thumbs-up, how can I complain?"

Olivia wished she could remember a funny character, some interesting turn of plot. All that had stuck was the book's "idea": Jesus, too, had been one of the homeless. To turn callously away from the homeless of today was exactly the same as turning away from Him. Informed of this alleged parallel, Dee had batted his eyes in theatrical disbelief. "Mary and Joe *homeless*? I never *heard* of such a thing! They had a perfectly *lovely* home on one of Nazareth's nicest streets. Yes, yes, they took their little trip to Bethlehem. But once their business with the tax men and the Wise Men was over, what did they do? *They went home.* Goodness heavens, how people *twist* things!"

Lori was checking her watch. "Boy's meeting me at the house right now, to show me around. My first time. It's terrible, but I never got to any of those World Harmony seminars they were always . . . Oh, my gosh! Olivia! You should come with me. It's right up your alley, and Boy's a character. He's a year younger than me, but he comes across like this crabby old . . . well, you'll see. I'm working on him. You don't develop your people skills, I tell him, no way you'll pull this off without bloodshed."

2

Boy Lyman was over six feet tall, with a caved-in chest and stooped, narrow shoulders. He had a long, flat-cheeked face, receding brown hair, and the slack middle that goes with sedentary habits. His shelter might be confrontational, but his clothes suggested residual tribal loyalties: worn tweed jacket, baggy chinos short in the leg, a skinny, rather greasy, striped tie.

Offering Olivia no contact with his pale eyes, he stuck out his hand.

She gave him hers and instantly regretted it. Boy had overlearned the principle of the firm handshake.

"I thought you were coming alone," he said to Lori.

At this loutishness, Olivia felt free to massage her metacarpals.

Lori gestured impatiently. "Spur of the moment. Olivia runs a very successful decorating business. She's got great ideas. And remember what I said about going with the flow? Remember in *3 Hots* when Spike showed up with the Sheetrock team? And Marilyn had to eat her words?"

"Right right right. Okay, fine, come on in. The more the merrier, as they say. But . . ." Head cocked, he studied Lori from head to toe. "Did you get a haircut or something?"

Lori giggled. "Or something. Do you like it?"

Boy blushed right up to his thinning roots. "It's really different."

Lori giggled some more. "Thanks, Boy. Now let's see the house."

The chill air, long unstirred, smelled of mildew and mice. The large foyer had a grimy marble floor and dark mahogany wainscoting that continued up the monumental staircase. To the left of the foyer was the grand salon. Plaster cherubs in varying stages of amputation flew garlands around the high ceiling. Bronze sconces, those that still had working bulbs, provided the dim lighting. "My grandmother was crazy about music," Boy said. "She'd invite these name-brand performers and stack the place nine deep with her friends. That door back there goes to the conservatory. Palms and whatnot, used to be."

"I'd love to see it," said Olivia.

"It's empty. Leaks like a sieve. I doubt that door's been opened in years."

"Bo-oy." Lori sang her warning playfully, but the message was clear.

"Right right right." He fussed through his bunch of keys, found the right one, shoved the door open.

Olivia caught her breath. Someone had fallen hard for Brighton Pavilion. The room was a filigreed hexagon, tiny, lead-framed panes, much broken, forming both the walls and the charming pagoda roof. The surviving floor tiles were a brilliant mandarin red.

"See what I mean?" Boy demanded. "Demolition city."

"Have you thought of selling it?" Olivia asked.

"This? Who'd want it?"

"One of the thousands of brand-new millionaires our wonderful American economy generates every year. Big new money equals big new houses, friends, behaviors. Someone's sure to want to offset all that raw upheaval with a beautiful old garden room. Also, think about breaking it up, selling sections. I had some clients who hated draperies, curtains of any kind. I used pieces of antique wrought-iron fencing around their windows, but this would have been even better."

Eye contact at last.

"I told you she had great ideas," said Lori.

On the other side of the foyer was the library, shelves empty, rich walnut paneling nicked and scarred. "What happened to the books?" Olivia asked. "And the furniture?"

"Grams wasn't really into antiques, so the furniture wasn't much. Anyway, the way it worked, my sisters' kids got the contents, I got the house."

Boy's smirk told Olivia all she needed to know about the fairness of this distribution. Behind the library was the dining room, hand-printed wallpaper and a splendid marble mantelpiece. "Someone stole the chandelier," Boy said. "That's a dumbwaiter. The kitchen's downstairs. Nothing to see."

"Show us anyway," Lori said.

Cavelike squalor. Olivia felt her shoes sticking to the floor. Sticky-looking walls, too—you could walk right up them like the Human Fly. The gas stove had those funny cabriole legs. Miles away from it, with no connecting countertop, was a shallow soapstone sink. Miles in the other direction, again freestanding, was a small refrigerator. For light, one tiny fluorescent ring in the center of the room.

Boy tugged at more doors. "Coal cellar. Wine. Laundry. Pantry."

They went back upstairs. The second floor was an enormous master bedroom and three smaller ones. There was one bathroom, tiled in white with black trim. Tiny octagons on the floor; flat, oversized squares on the walls. The huge clawfooted tub had more old rings than Firestone and Parson, specialists in estate jewelry. The chain-pull toilet was unspeakable; the stray hair clumping everywhere would stuff a sofa pillow.

The third floor had a twin of this bathroom and five more

bedrooms. Each had a fireplace with a marble mantelpiece and coal grate. "Hardly used," said Boy. "You'd get a bedroom fire if you were real sick, I guess. Otherwise never. Warm bedrooms were conducive to flabby morals. Even when they got central heating, in the late thirties, they'd turn the radiators off at night."

The warren of cells that constituted the fourth-floor servants' quarters had neither fireplaces nor radiators. No bathroom either, just a filthy toilet in a windowless closet.

"What did they do for heat?" Lori asked.

"Bundled," suggested Olivia. "Two to a bed."

"When they did the central heating," Boy said, "the contractor quoted Gram a price for radiators on all four floors. 'I don't understand,' she goes, real puzzled. 'Nobody's up there but Irish.'"

"That's horrible," said Lori. "I'm part Irish myself."

"Yeah, well, what can you expect from slavers? Want to hear something amazing? These bedrooms are slightly bigger than the mandated SRO standard. I find that hard to believe."

Olivia thought she might as well ask a professional's question. "Will tenants have their own bathrooms and kitchens?"

"Guests, we're calling them," said Lori.

"We have to run the numbers," said Boy, "see what's possible. The game plan is to stick with rooming-house rules. That's what this joint is, you know. Gramps got it licensed so the harmonists could sleep in."

"Which is an incredibly lucky break," said Lori. "Rooming houses are sacred cows, maybe even on Chestnut Street. But we've *got* to give everyone a bathroom, Boy. People in *jail* have their own toilets."

"Yeah, well. Have to see."

"And kitchens. Otherwise they'll do hot plates, set the place on fire. Plus, ever try to wash pots and pans in a bathroom sink? Well, I have. Plumbing problems you wouldn't believe. Not to mention roaches and rats."

"Like I said, it's financial."

Lori let fly. "How'm I going to blow up this balloon if you keep sticking in pins?"

Boy blinked in surprise. "Why're you yelling?"

"You won't dream, that's why! You quit before you start!"

"There's only so much money. We've got to be realistic."

"Defeatist, you mean."

"That's not fair. I'm hung way out on this thing. I'm totally, *totally* committed. Ask the people next door. Ask across the street. You know Peter Robertson? Big hotshot litigator, gets five, six hundred an hour? He goes around saying I'm the most stubborn son of a bitch he's ever had the sorrow to deal with."

"Yeah?" Lori was delighted. "That's great, Boy. Really terrific. So why not be stubborn on bathrooms and kitchens? Bold up, for God's sake. Dare to dream. Empower yourself!"

"And the money just drops out of the sky?"

"Jeezies, Boy! You're obsessed. Too bad you didn't have my advantages, growing up."

"I thought you grew up, you know, poor." Then, Lori and Olivia both laughing: "Oh. I get it."

"Fine. So what's your homework assignment?"

"A wish list?"

"Fine again. And after that? When you're talking to one of your richie neighbors, say?"

"I hit them with my dream." He made a fist, punched air. "Right between the eyes."

"And?"

"And what? Oh, wait, I know. I adapt, go with the flow."

"Excellent. You might also consider telling Mr. Robertson and the rest that you're launching neighborhood fund-raising. And don't give me that look. It's in their own best interests. The shelter's going to happen no matter what, but their generosity will lift it above the norm. Make it the best SRO the world has ever seen. A model we can all be proud of."

"They'll laugh in my face."

"I bet they'll feel defensive, put on the spot. Whatever they usually do to handle those feelings—laugh, get mad, cry poor—they'll do to you. Let them. You've got the moral high ground and they'll know it. Basically you're issuing an invitation. You're like, 'Hey guys, you want the high ground too? Love to have you up here with me, just bring your checkbook.' "

"You make it sound so easy."

Lori stamped her foot. "It *is* easy. Define your dream and believe in it with all your heart. The rest is details."

Olivia watched hope chase wariness around Boy's face. Then, wistfully: "I just wish you'd do it with me."

"I am. I'm on the board. You sign up anyone else yet?"

"I'm working on it. What I mean is, I wish you'd come along when I'm talking to people."

"I told you. My tour is twelve days, plus collapse time when I get back. After which I've got to sit down and write my army book. It's not the kind of work you can delegate, writing."

"Right right right. Sorry. I only thought . . ."

"You'll do fine. Don't forget, you're the one who got Michelle Greene all fired up."

Olivia was impressed. Michelle Greene was, by any standard, a coup. The architect for some of the city's classiest office towers, she'd also worked wonders in the penny-pinch realm of low-income housing.

Boy had an idea. "What if I had your itinerary? So I could fax you things."

"Better not. These tours are zooey. It's hard to focus."

"Then let's go have lunch. So I can kind of get a head start, rough out some ideas with you."

"Lunch at nine-thirty?"

"Coffee, then. I missed breakfast."

"All right. I'm all dressed up, might as well go someplace. How about you, Olivia?"

Olivia waited an extra beat before putting Boy out of his misery. "Thanks, no. I'm due back at my office."

And how delicious, she thought as she walked home, that nothing was forcing her to pitch this job, either by buttering up Boy or finagling an encounter with Michelle Greene.

The last time the trees had turned, Olivia's finances had been very different. Philip's health insurance had covered only a fraction of the nursing home, and no one could predict how much longer he'd be there. Her in-laws had helped, but most of the pressure had been on her. She took on more work than she could comfortably handle, and if landing a job obliged her to butter up and finagle, she would.

Compared to then, she was now a woman of means; Philip had had terrific *life* insurance. A woman of means need not kiss ass. Ever.

Even if she sometimes cried herself to sleep, she'd have to call that progress.

At six-thirty that evening, Dee joined Olivia in her skylit top floor—originally servants' bedrooms, just as at Boy's house. Olivia and Philip hadn't anticipated live-in servants, but in any case, why squander sun on rooms used mostly at night? They'd gutted the walls, fitted the large, airy space with what was needed for cooking, eating, conversation, reading, listening to music. ("No TV," Philip had decreed. "You kids want to watch TV, go downstairs. You too, Olivia." His theory: TV, infernal polluter, would lose audience if unsupported by companionship, music, refrigerator, and hearth.) A circular staircase led to a roof deck, another reason to reverse the configuration normal to these tall old houses. Who'd ever cook in a first-floor kitchen, then hike everything up and up to eat al fresco?

From the time Dee had moved in, right after the accident, he and Olivia would get together weekly, sometimes his place, sometimes hers. If the host hadn't cooked, they'd order take-out of some description.

This had gone on so long that Olivia tended to forget how unusual such easy sociability was. Propinquity was a factor, she supposed. So was the long duration of their friendship. That her largesse figured at all—the rent she charged Dee was only what a serious writer and part-time college instructor could afford—she refused to contemplate.

Philip's parents had been vocal in their disapproval of Dee's tenancy. Abbott and Ryland, Olivia should remember, were at a *very impressionable* age. She should give *very serious thought* to the example she was setting. The day they'd buried Philip, his mother had said, "At least you can have your house back."

Olivia wanted it articulated. "What do you mean, Sally?"

"You don't need that rental income anymore."

"True. But Dee still needs an affordable place to live."

Sally's eyes narrowed. Philip had been her only child, and Olivia had let him die. Entirely and outrageously on her own authority, she had presumed to say no to the drug that might have prolonged his parents' hopes for a miracle. "Such a soft heart," she said, spitting the words.

Olivia tried reason. "Dee's my oldest friend. Philip's too."

"Don't you *dare* bring my son into this. Where was your soft heart when it came to *him*? Hard as *nails*, that's where."

Dee drank his invariable beer, Dos Equis; Olivia, white wine. Mikey's presumed rumor and her house tour had absorbed their first round.

Olivia's preference for white bullets, which was what Pip, her father-in-law, called vodka on the rocks, had ended with summer. She'd been pouring herself a blithe pre-dinner fourth when, no warning, a big bright light went on. Panic shaking her hand, she emptied her glass into the sink. Didn't touch a drop for days, not until she was sure she knew where she was.

Now she drank wine only and, most of the time, paid attention to how much.

"Tell me more about Boy," Dee said, topping himself up. "He's for real? Your basic Boston do-gooder?"

"I guess. With loutish edges. Or do I mean oafish? Lori says he's tormented by the triangle trade. That's what built the Lyman house in the first place, and it's basically what's funding Boy today."

"Slaves in Africa," Dee said, starting a triangle in the air; "sugar cane in the Caribbean; what's the third leg?"

"Rum here. They converted the sugar into molasses— where, I don't know."

"Which leg did Boy's people work?"

"The worst," Olivia said. "He referred to them as slavers. But don't discount the other triangular crimes. The sugar plantations wiped out the forests of the Caribbean. Enter chronic drought, topsoil depletion and runoff, plus the plant diseases and pests attendant on one-crop agribiz."

"Environmental guilt. How modish."

"Substance-abuse guilt, too," Olivia reminded him. "The rum aspect."

"Right. We do call them rummies, don't we? Not whiskies or"—his eyes slid away from hers—"vodkies."

Olivia saluted him with her glass. "*I* call them winos."

"Oops."

"Don't preach to the converted," she said. "Waste of energy."

"You're right. Forgive, please. Let's go back to Boy."

"Let's. According to Lori, his grandfather was hoping he'd join the World Harmonists. Boy pleaded restlessness and got the old peacenik to foot his wanderings—Africa, India, Tibet, your basic Third World hegira. Guess what brought him home?"

She gave Lori's version, sparing Dee the guessing game. "*3 Hots & a Cot*," she concluded, "joined Boy to his ordained destiny. And revealed to him the natural destiny of the Lyman house."

Dee groaned. "To paraphrase Cole Porter, one must never underestimate the potency of cheap fiction."

"Did you read it? No? Not even after I tempted you with the homeless Christ Child?"

"Writers who don't make enough money *never* read writers who make too much. I've sampled a few pages of the Lutz oeuvre; to do more would be physically impossible."

"I see." Olivia smiled. "Envy plays no role here?"

"Envy plays a role everywhere, and it's much aggravated by Lori's heavy-handed reliance on the adverb. But I lie. In spite of myself, I've enjoyed the occasional best-seller. There's an analogy to junk food. It's all bad for you, but some's yummy, like McDonald's fries, and some's cardboard, like Twinkies. My scannings confirm that Lori does Twinkies. By the way, you've explained a minor mystery. She's not much for good works, Lori. I've tried to get her to get involved here and there—Artists for Peace, for AIDS, a freedom-of-expression panel. No dice. She'll send a check, but she's on deadline, can't spare a second. Now I see my mistake. Next time I'll approach as Boy did, with book hugged to heart."

"If all she does is Twinkies, why approach her at all?"

"Why else? She's a name. A star. A major draw."

Olivia had a thought. "Does her husband get involved in causes?"

"Rob Mallory, Beantown's greatest one-book author? No, but who cares? She's the crowd-pleaser, not him."

"I wonder what it's like, being them."

"Yes," said Dee. "His slender output and great prestige, her critically scorned but profitable prolixity. I didn't exactly like *Perfectly Honest*, but I admired it. I must read it again someday, see if it's been squashed flat by the awesome burden it's had to bear."

"Burden?"

"Justifying Rob's existence."

"Want to hear a confession?" Olivia asked.

"Always."

"When they lived on Joy Street, I'd spy on them. It was lunchtime here, but they'd be eating breakfast on their deck. He'd be deep in his paper, paying no attention to her. After a while she'd jump up, start deadheading the petunias or something. No reaction from him, so she'd work her way around to the door. The second she's about to open it and go inside, he drops his paper and starts talking to her. Reels her in, couple of steps at a time, until she's sitting down again, ready to talk. Before she can say much, he's back into his paper. Then the cycle would start all over again. It took her three, four tries before she could finally escape. Gave me the creeps. It was as if he had her on a choke chain."

"You got a problem with the naked exercise of dominance?"

"*Faked* exercise, you mean. The dominant one was Lori. If she didn't get to her desk, they wouldn't eat. What's so funny?"

Dee grinned. "I love it when you get all healthy-minded and practical."

"Okay, they're into bondage. I only saw the foreplay. The real fun started later, after he chained her to her desk."

"I had a simpler dominance in mind," Dee said. "He's an artist, she's a craftsperson."

"That gives him license to jerk her around?"

"Plenty. Especially considering the known biography. I ever tell you I met a guy who lived with Rob and Lori in the old days? You sure? Okay, but stop me if it's a rerun. This guy and Rob and some other Harvards decide to stay together after graduation. They hang out at a greasy spoon called the Agora and their favorite waitress is Lori. They decide to adopt her, bring her home. They've been worried they're too elitist. They think Lori will infuse their lives with the deep wisdom of the common folk.

"Time passes, and Lori falls madly in love with Rob. She copies everything he does—wears his shirts, puts her hair in the same kind of ponytail, gets glasses like his, plain lenses because there's nothing wrong with her eyes. She even spends her time off from the Agora the same way he does, yellow pad and pencil, scribble, scribble, scribble.

"He's dedicated, Rob. A driven creature. 'Slow down, man,' the others say, 'ease off, give yourself a break.' He gives them the burning eyes, the white-knuckled grip on the chair arms. 'I'm either going to *write*'—full stop, portentous-like—'or *kill* myself.'

"More time passes. Rob's itchy, needs space. Flees to Mexico, address unknown. Lori keeps scribbling. By the time Rob's home again, *Home Cooking*, her restaurant novel, is a runaway best-seller and she's working on her second. They marry and move to Joy Street so you can watch their breakfast games, and Rob, for the first time in his life, can write full-time.

"Pretty soon, *Perfectly Honest* comes out, so-so sales, great acclaim. Lori's second book comes out, too."

"*3 Hots & a Cot*," said Olivia.

"None other. It doesn't even come close to meeting its disgustingly superfatted advance. No matter; Hollywood has taken *Home Cooking* to its heart. The movie's a hit; the enriched couple buy their house on Mount Vernon; we Joy Street proles are left in the dust."

Olivia recalled something. "Lori was strange when I asked her if he was going on her book tour. Maybe he's got better things to do. Maybe he's putting the finishing touches on a book that's going to outdo *Perfectly Honest*—which, by the way, I never read."

"How come?"

"Philip and I decided to boycott it. Rob used to come up to one or the other of us at some neighborhood party and then cruise the room over our shoulders. Looking for someone more important to talk to. You reject adverbs, we rejected that."

"I reject it too," said Dee. "It's hateful. His book has hateful aspects too, though the basic premise is intriguing. The protagonist, Kurt, believes that the greatest good in life is freedom from self-deception."

"Keep talking. I've got to stir our chili."

Dee followed her into the kitchen. "Kurt, a neurotic mess, impregnates his girlfriend. Fearing that the baby will be harmed by the load of bad he's carrying around from his own unloved childhood, he goes into therapy. The couple marry, have two more kids. Because Kurt's been shrunk, he's able to help all three achieve a degree of self-assurance and esteem he never had. What do you suppose happens?"

"Nothing good," Olivia knew.

"Right. The kids turn out wonderfully free of neurosis and wonderfully free of anything resembling an interesting personality. Which is okay with the mom—she's underdrawn, to put it mildly—but they bore the pants off Kurt. He can hardly bear to be in the same room with them. The kids' boringness is very well done. In case you don't know, it's extremely difficult to make boredom real on the page without boring the reader."

"Is it funny?" Olivia asked.

"Sometimes. I think the phrase would be *biting wit*. The mom takes the two younger kids away for the summer, leaving Kurt alone with the oldest, who's thirteen. He starts torturing her. Little stuff at first, the kind of thing you used to spy on, then sexual teasing, then serious sadism."

"Horrible," said Olivia.

"He's trying to break through. He's sure there's something buried deep within his daughter that won't bore him, but before he can locate it she dies."

"How?"

"Sure you want to know? She's strangled. One of his bondage games goes wrong. Hey. I warned you. What's amazing is the way Kurt retains a hold on your sympathy. Like the Peter Lorre character in *M*."

"So what's the moral? Don't go into therapy?"

"No moral. It's a work of art."

"Oh."

"And we mustn't confuse what a man writes about with what he is. Books are not life."

"Boy Lyman thinks they are," Olivia reminded him.

"*We* are not Boy Lyman."

"True. I like Lori. I'm glad Rob had that vasectomy, and I hope he's nicer to her than I think he is."

Dee gave a Latin shrug. "The impenetrable secrets of marriage! Whatever else, we can be sure he's still writing."

"We can?"

"Hasn't killed himself, has he?"

3

The Manhattan wedding of Josie Spangler, Olivia's last and best assistant, went like clockwork but was much more fun.

"How's my replacement working out?" asked the bride.

"I haven't hired anybody," Olivia told her. "And not only because you spoiled me. I'm down to one client—that penthouse job, remember?"

Great alarm. "Don't tell me you're closing shop."

"I'm picking and choosing. I've got to like the whole package—people, project, location, everything. So far nothing's tempted me. Also, I need a vacation."

Josie wasn't reassured. "What about when the vacation's over? Will you do three-hour lunches? Hang around the Design Center like some amateur from the burbs?"

"Amateurs work for the love of it. That's what the word means."

"Well. You can always go back."

To the real thing, Josie obviously meant. Seven months on Central Park West had made her a New Yorker. The toughest, fastest, most competitive route was the only way to go. Everything else reeked of gutless compromise.

* * *

Back in Boston, emerging from the airport subway at Government Center, Olivia was hard hit by culture shock. Against New York's teeming complexities, Boston seemed an overgrown village. City Hall's vast brick-paved plaza, empty except for scraps of blowing trash, had never looked more barren or stupid.

The sky was a rich, glowing coral—courtesy, Olivia had read, of dust from the latest volcanic belch. She sighed, shifted her duffel strap to a less bony place on her shoulder, and began the short walk home.

Nothing like a wedding to activate the who-you-gonna-love-who's-gonna-love-you blues. A woman living in an overgrown village knows precisely where all the good men her age are spending their Sunday evenings—at home with wives or lovers. Manhattan, big and busy, was different. Living there would be like bicycling along a winding, hilly road, tempted onward by the possibility of novelty, astonishment, delight, around the next bend. In a village everything was predictable. You cycled a level, featureless straightaway, no surprises on either side, nothing in the distance but the vanishing point of the horizon.

No surprises included no bad ones, of course. Boston did feel safer than New York. But so what, if it only translated into boredom and predictability?

Ahead was one of her favorite urban compositions, upper Mount Vernon. Framed by the arch of the State House passageway, the houses, subtly punctuated by gaslights, rose elegantly to meet the radiant coral of the sky.

"Bah, humbug," muttered Olivia.

A couple entered the other end of the passageway, dawdling toward her. Lovers, she enviously guessed. Their only touch was fingers lightly linked, but there was no mistaking that rapt absorption. Both wore jeans, the man a leather bomber jacket, the woman an Armani-like topcoat. They were about the same height, which emphasized their closeness.

Closer, she recognized Rob Mallory. Lori, of course, was still away on her book tour. Even so, it was pretty dumb of Rob to appear so obviously smitten. Villagers notice; villagers talk.

Olivia kept her eyes straight ahead. If he didn't speak, she wouldn't either.

Not only did he greet her, he made a point of it, pausing as if eager to chat. The woman moved on a few steps, made a half-turn, waited. She was a tomboy type, slim and fit, quite young. She had a decisive nose, a mop of curly dark hair, blue eyes emphasized by heavy mascara, and a flowery blue scarf tied around her neck. Odd choice, flowered chiffon. Wrong for Armani, not to mention tomboy.

Rob indicated Olivia's duffel. "Been away?"

"For the weekend. New York."

"Lucky you got out alive. Meet Kim Amundsen, Olivia. Like the explorer."

"Hi," said Olivia.

Kim nodded. None of this, her aloof smile said, has anything to do with me.

Olivia switched her bag to her other shoulder. "See you around," she said.

Rob wasn't quite through. "Soon as Lori gets back," he said, "I'll have her give you a jingle. That wreck we call home is really getting to us. I mean, it's not like we're students anymore. We've got to bite the bullet, start fixing up."

Olivia sneaked a look at Kim. Her detached smile wobbled. Hurt? Jealousy?

Rob's implication was much clearer. If Olivia was working for him, she'd keep her mouth shut on his cheating.

Olivia almost told him to take his house and stuff it sideways. More strategic, though, to boost the aggrieved wife. "I'd love to hear from Lori. Whatever the subject."

Kim's smile vanished. Rob made hearty noises. Olivia made tracks.

* * *

Approaching home, Olivia saw that the second-floor windows were dark. Dee must be out. Or in bed. (All the good men are married or gay.)

The brass fittings on the front door had been polished very recently. Inside, the little foyer shone with cleanliness. Dee's work. Also his idea, bartering housekeeping chores in exchange for the break Olivia gave him on his rent. So far, the only problem with the arrangement had been a secret one of her own—her fading but still pesky impulse, upon hearing the vacuum, to jump up, lend the poor man a hand. It surprised her, this residue of throwback femininity. She saw the funny side, but it was embarrassing, getting caught out like that.

She paused at the foot of the staircase. Check the messages on her office phone? Let them wait until morning?

As if to settle the debate, a phone began to ring—the tinny personal one, not the full-bodied business line.

"Mrs. Chapman? It's Will Barkhorn, up at Cheshire."

Her younger son Ryland's housemaster. Sunday, this hour, it might be trouble. "Something came to my attention, and I thought we should touch base," he said. "Ryland has quit the soccer team."

Relief washed through her. With wild-card Ryland, you never knew. But why did Barkhorn sound so doomful? "Isn't that good? Last time we spoke we decided he should put more into Latin and math, less into sports."

"Well, that's just it, Mrs. Chapman. This has nothing to do with studies. I'm afraid he has simply switched extracurricular horses, if you will, in midstream. Taken your advice for an end run."

What advice? Ryland had marched to his own drum since infancy. A kid like that, you pick your fights. She'd never waste her energy and prestige on extracurriculars. But to ask Barkhorn for specifics might trip Ryland up, and that she must not do. One of Philip's cardinal principles had been that kids away at school deserve fierce and seamless loyalty from their parents. Schools, he'd said, can be trusted only to educate, not love. Until Olivia could speak to Ryland directly, she'd have to hedge. "And does the new horse require as much time as the old one?"

"The new . . . Oh. Sorry. I'm afraid so. Especially in the last few weeks before the performance. But time isn't really the issue, Mrs. Chapman. Ryland was a starter, of course, so by dropping out in midseason he's letting the whole team down. Perhaps you weren't aware of that when you advised him. Not that *The Mikado* isn't great fun. I sang in it myself. I was Peep-Bo—this was back before coeducation, of course. Well. I just wanted to make sure we're all rowing with the same kind of oar, if you will. I can understand why you'd encourage Ryland in the arts, but I'm sure you'll agree this should be his decision, not someone else's."

Best not mention, Olivia thought, that she, too, had sung Peep-Bo in high school. "I agree completely. Soon as we hang up, I'm going to call him on the dorm phone."

"Fine. Let me know if you can't get through. He's welcome to call from here."

Where you can hear every word he says? "Thanks. I'll get back to you soon."

She didn't call Ryland right away. Couldn't. Too angry. Damn, Philip! If we can't trust these people to love him, why's he in their hands? Why'd you talk me into sending him away in the first place?

Okay, Okay. If Ryland lived with her twenty-four hours a day, there'd be problems too—different ones, probably, but no guarantees they'd be simpler. Because wasn't it Ryland's *job* to wrangle with his environment? To test and stretch himself? Did she want a gray little Milquetoast, a spiritless automaton capable only of getting and spending and watching TV? So. *Her* job was to love and support him, especially when he was making mistakes. And telling lies.

"Hi, Ryland."

"Mom! Hi!"

"I've just been talking to Mr. Barkhorn about *The Mikado*."

"Oh. He called you?"

"Yes. What's your part?"

"Nanki-Poo."

The tenor lead. "Goodness, Ry. Congratulations. You constantly surprise me."

"It's neat, Mom. I really get to ham it up. The director says it's totally impossible to overact when you do Gilbert and Sullivan."

"I can't wait to see for myself. Why does Mr. Barkhorn think I advised you to quit soccer?"

Silence in Cheshire. Olivia was determined to wait her son out.

"I guess I sort of said you did."

"Mind telling me why?"

"Oh, God. Basically on account of the guys. The team, Mom. They'd crucify me if they knew the real reason."

"Which is?"

"Soccer's so boring! Last year it was a big deal, getting on the first string and all. But now I'm like, okay, I did that, what else do I want to do? I mean, baseball's my real sport. Just because I turned out to be halfway decent at soccer, do I have to play it for the rest of my *life*?"

"No. But that's not the explanation Cheshire got, right? What exactly did you say?"

More silence. Then, with a heavy sigh: "Basically I told them you were crazy about Gilbert and Sullivan. Which is true, right?"

"Right. And?"

"And this was a real hard time for you, so I wanted to, you know, do something that would sort of cheer you up."

Shit. He'd used family grief. Scuttled beneath its soft underbelly instead of standing his ground.

On the other hand, it was a hard time for him, too.

On the other hand, he'd lied.

Not to her. At least he wasn't lying to her.

"I had to say *something*, Mom. The kids in theater are, you know, on the artsy side. One guy is definitely gay, and some of the others . . ."

"Is that a problem for you?"

"Nah. I'm like Dad. Cool. Except . . . everyone knows about Dee, Mom. Jill told. People've have been, like"—he moved into lisping falsetto—"'Eeew-ie, I'm not going near *your* house, that stuff's *contagious.*'"

Jill had been Ryland's girlfriend last summer. Meeting Dee, she'd fallen under the spell of his dark good looks and flirted shamelessly. Olivia felt a stab of fury. "Lots of people are saying things like this?"

"It's mostly the jocks."

"And what do you say?"

"Nothing. I blow it off. They're ignorant, Mom. Bad as Grammy and Gramps. They're not going to listen to a lecture from me."

"Yeah. All right. I'm going to sleep on this. Call me early tomorrow morning, and then I'll call Barkhorn."

"You gonna say I lied?"

"Right there, Ryland, right what you're thinking and feeling this exact minute is what I hope you'll remember about this business. You put me in a bad position. I'm your mother, so my instinct is to protect you. Against that, I don't want to sanction your lying. Okay, that's the bind I'm sleeping on. You sleep on it too."

After they said good-bye, Olivia slumped in her desk chair, her body heavy and tired, headache throbbing behind her eyes. Uncanny how kid problems always struck when you were low to begin with.

No footsteps sounded from above. Dee, the one person she could trust to care about Ryland almost as much as she did, was unavailable. And also, no fault of his own, part of the problem.

Because almost certainly Barkhorn and the rest of the teachers and staff—the "we" who were so "concerned" about Ryland's recent behavior—now believed that the Chapman roof sheltered a dangerous exotic. Add it up, one or another of these worthies would have proposed. Single mother, openly gay friend, all manner of *his* friends coming and going, Ryland meeting them, and so forth. And now rugged, manly soccer jettisoned in favor of song and dance. The good fun of *The Mikado* notwithstanding, we better move on this one before it's too late.

She wearily supposed Cheshire's biases might have been anticipated and prepared for. On the bright side, Ryland could have dealt with his problem in ways far more troubling. He could have blamed his mother for Dee, cursed the day Dee had come into their lives. Instead, he seemed to have divided the world into good guys, himself among them, and homophobic ignoramuses.

Including his grandparents.

That Jill. How dare she describe Dee as anything less than the very soul of responsible restraint? She'd thrown everything she had at the man, and what had he done? Given her the full benefit of his lengthy experience with flirts of all sexes, that's what. Eased her off with courtly grace, every shred of her young dignity intact.

Moral midgets, all of them. Grabbing for scapegoats instead of confronting their fears and weaknesses. She hated to admit it, but Rob Mallory's horrid book was onto something. Freedom from self-deception might not be life's absolute greatest good, but it was right up there. And certainly its unfree opposite was a contender for greatest troublemaker.

4

Olivia was working in her office by the time Ryland called. Earlier would have been better, but when in his life had Ryland ever managed to be early?

"I couldn't get to sleep last night," he said. "I kept thinking and thinking. And then this morning I didn't hear the first bell."

Olivia hastened to put him out of his misery. "I'm telling Mr. Barkhorn I'm convinced you picked theater over soccer all by yourself. No pressure from me or anyone else."

"I don't get it."

Olivia didn't blame him. Distracted by her insights into the school's anxieties, she'd been slow to get it herself. Clarity had come with a morning realization: Since Barkhorn and the rest were being evasive, neither she nor Ryland were obliged to be entirely direct. "Mr. Barkhorn's afraid you're too much under my thumb. He must not know you very well."

"Yeah, but Mom. What about Dee and all?"

"That only came up between you and me. Mr. Barkhorn never said a word."

"Yeah, but it's practically the whole reason—"

"You'll handle this, Ry. You've done fine so far, except for putting words in my mouth. So modify a little. You were hoping I'd be pleased, and I am, but after we talked last night you realized the choice *of pleasing me* was entirely your own. And it was, right? The rest is your business, no one else's. It'll blow over. You keep delivering the exact same line, the people pestering you will get tired of hearing it and move on. Concentrate on this: You're way ahead because you're more relaxed about human complexity. You're able to see Dee as he really is and enjoy his company. No panics, no running scared."

"Okay, but I gotta say it, Mom. They're not all like him, gays."

"No. The world's not so nice a place. Have fun singing, Ry. I love you."

"Love you too."

She dialed Barkhorn, got his machine, delivered her lines. Still smiling with satisfaction, she heard Dee getting out his bicycle, stored with hers in the back room that had been the kitchen in the 1840s, when the house was new. Monday mornings, if she remembered correctly, he taught at MIT.

He peered in, saw her smile. "So merry?" he asked. "From a wedding?"

Dee didn't do weddings. Until AIDS, he hadn't done funerals either.

"I liked it," she told him. "Nice people, delicious food, no sense of doom during the vows."

"Huh."

"How was your weekend?"

"Kevin took me on a foliage tour."

"And?"

"Nature's chromatic extravagance was good for an hour or so. Otherwise it was white-bread. But then, so is Kevin."

Olivia ignored this. Kevin was cute and monumentally dumb. Why he continued to interest Dee was a mystery she'd quit trying to fathom. "Foilage, Abbott used to say."

"I'd forgotten that. We all picked it up. Why'd we ever stop?"

"He decided we were making fun of him."

"Youth. It really is wasted on them, isn't it? Speaking of such, my engineers await me. Big treat today: How to find a lifelong friend in the subordinate clause."

If only, Olivia suddenly wished, Cheshire could see Dee right this minute. What if she invited him up for Ryland's performance?

The idea had no sooner formed than she axed it. Dee was too good a man to be roped into show-and-tell. Cheshire could either save itself or stumble on blind. She'd given them Ryland, and that was enough. Infinitely more than they deserved.

Olivia spent the last half of Wednesday afternoon in the Back Bay with Steven Dunbar, the rich bachelor she'd been working with since last spring. His penthouse, on the coveted water side of Beacon, had generated some novel challenges. To support a major Jacuzzi, the floor had to be reinforced. So that bathers could enjoy the panoramic river view, a fog-proofing system had to be devised for the windows. Dunbar had been very specific: "I don't want a living room that looks like a health club. I don't want that chemical smell. Unless the tub's in use, it has to be totally invisible. A surprise I can unveil at the psychological moment."

Of seduction, he meant. Dunbar was a fool for love.

Today's meeting introduced a new demand: Olivia must incorporate the talents of his new girlfriend, a specialist in faux finishes, into the existing design scheme. "Val's terrific, Olivia. I want to give her a free rein. Use the place to showcase her."

Dunbar's girlfriends had a high rate of turnover. Even if Olivia were to conquer her dislike for unbridled faux, there were no guarantees that Val would stay the course. Complicating matters further, Dunbar had once offered Olivia girlfriend status, which she'd declined.

"Showcase yes, free rein no," she said. "As long as Val understands I'm in charge, I'm sure we can work things out."

Looking much beleaguered, Dunbar said he'd get back to her.

It was almost dark when Olivia started home. Short days were the worst of winter. You could convince yourself cold was bracing, but how to take a positive view of vanishing light?

As she cycled up to the crest of Joy, bulging barriers of black and green plastic bags reminded her that tomorrow was trash day. Three times a week this curbside spew occurred. Three times a week she marveled at the volume.

She stowed her bike and, as was her custom, started picking up today's Dunkin' Donuts cups and the rest of the junk people had chucked around her front door. Fact of American life: You live in a tourist trap, you get fast-food mess.

Stooping, she sensed someone trying to pass.

It was Lori Lutz, back in her sweatpants. A knitted poncho with ratty fringe covered one arm. From the other dangled a plastic Stop and Shop bag.

They exchanged greetings. Olivia wanted to ask about the book tour, but Lori got in first. "My arm's in a sling. I fell changing a ceiling bulb, and they say it's a sprained wrist."

"And of course you're right-handed."

"Of course." She gave her head a despairing shake. "I just wish I could come up with a punch line. You know, how many klutzy novelists does it take to change a lightbulb?" Her laugh was loud but mirthless.

"What a shame. How are you at dictating?"

"Not good. I get self-conscious. Listen, Olivia, I was going to call you. When I got home from the tour, Rob told me you were expecting us to—" She broke off, swallowed, tried again. "He said— Oh, God."

Tears welled, spilled down her cheeks. The grocery bag hit

the sidewalk with a sound of breaking glass. She hid her face behind her good arm and shook with stifled sobs.

"Come in, sit down a minute," Olivia said. What had happened to upset her? Had the prospect of decorating, its connubial, long-term implications, driven Rob to reveal his girlfriend?

Opening the front door, Olivia guided the weeping woman to the bench just inside. "There. I'll grab your groceries, be right back."

Orange juice sloshed in the bottom of the bag. Olivia dumped as much as she could, set the sticky remainder on the foyer floor.

Lori was doubled over, crying hard. Olivia sat beside her. After a moment's hesitation—they weren't such close friends that this was natural—she laid her arm across the heaving shoulders.

Lori flinched away, cowered in abject fear. *Don't*, her body language screamed, *please don't hit me.* Too late she caught herself, met Olivia's astonishment with her own shock and alarm.

A wail of pure grief broke from her. Her secret betrayed by her own assaulted body, she collapsed utterly.

Offered tortellini con panna, Lori didn't think she could touch a bite. "Try," Olivia coaxed. "You should take painkillers with food." (Lori had tearfully revealed that her evening shopping had included some Percocet, more powerful than the drug she'd been prescribed initially.)

Once started, Lori ate hungrily. "More wine?" Olivia asked.

"Thanks. Though it'll probably put me under the table."

"Fine. You can sleep in one of the boys' beds."

Once again Lori told her how wonderful she was, how kind and sweet. Olivia, by now, was reduced to meeting this effusiveness with a forced smile. Her first response had been her truest: Nonsense, anyone would have done the same. Downgrade from there, and no way out. Lori's restoration was much too fragile for candor, for straight talk.

Rob Mallory was a batterer. Lori's sprained wrist was only the most obvious injury from last night's beating. The puffy jaw Olivia had noticed before her book tour had been the result of another fight. Over the years, Rob had thrown furniture at his wife, shoved her into walls and down flights of stairs. He had punched her stomach so hard she'd passed out. His blows to her head had bloodied her nose, left her with ringing and aching ears, loosened teeth, blackened eyes.

Shamed and humiliated, Lori had never breathed a word. Once started, she seemed possessed, fiercely determined to spell out every sickening detail. As the outrages piled up, Olivia found it more and more difficult to listen patiently. She wanted to take action, call the police. Rob was a monster. He should be charged, tried, locked up for life.

She shivered, remembering the breakfast games she'd spied on, Rob reeling her in, Lori's docility. And what about Rob's horrific novel? Art isn't life, Dee had said, but who'd dare believe that Rob's cruelty would stop at punching and shoving?

At this point, a new element was creeping into Lori's pell-mell spill. To each fresh confession of assault, she'd add a trailer of excuse, rationalization. "Parties like that, you always drink too much. . . . Rob's mother never touched him, never once. Isn't that unbelievable? Four children and she never hugged a one of them? Even when they were tiny babies? . . . Arguing with a man who's had that much to drink and God knows how many lines of coke—I should know better. . . . You know what I think it all comes down to? I've had success in the world and Rob hasn't. My tours, the coverage I get, the wining and dining, every bit of it twists the knife. Plus, I came home raring to write. That was Monday, and Tuesday morning I got right to it, had this really great time at my desk. A break-through, because this new book's been like pulling teeth. But look at Rob! No breakthroughs for years and years. This whole thing . . . you sort of have to . . . you know? Because how's he supposed to handle it?" Finally, grotesquely: "Thank God I celebrated my great writing day. If I hadn't gotten so loaded, I could've really hurt myself."

As Olivia sat speechless, Lori gave the table a decisive slap with her good hand. "I'd better call him." Then, as if wanting permission, "Okay?"

"Your decision, Lori."

"I won't say where I am. You won't be involved."

"I'm not worried about involvement." And so what if she were? Olivia thought tiredly. Anything Rob wanted to know, he'd beat it loose.

"The thing is, unless he knows I'm okay, he could feel forced to, you know, go public on this. Call our friends, not that we have that many, maybe even the police. Then when I show up, nothing wrong, I'll *really* be in trouble."

Lost cause, Olivia told herself. As she'd recently heard a man say in the Spa, you can't lead a dead horse to water. "Phone's over there. Or downstairs in my bedroom, if you'd rather."

She'd rather.

Olivia had cleaned up the kitchen by the time Lori returned. "That was definitely the right move," she announced. "He'd already called Boy Lyman and Mass. General, looking for me." A wan smile. "He wants me to come home."

"Does that surprise you?"

"Not really. He loves me. And I love him." Fresh tears shone in her eyes. "After all's said and done, that's where it's at. Rob is the man I love, the only man I've ever loved."

Olivia couldn't think of a thing to say. Not that it mattered. Lori was talking, not listening. Olivia had to understand, she urgently insisted, the nature of art's sacred demands. Rob was, above all, an artist. "With a capital *A*, I mean. Not like me."

Olivia had to interrupt. "What kind of artist are you?"

"Oh, you know. Strictly pop. Basically I try to give people

what they want. Rob's totally disinterested, wait, *un*interested—
wow, lucky he didn't hear that one. Anyway, he's not remotely
into what people like, what they expect, all that. He writes for
himself, period."

"Had Rob been drinking?"

"Excuse me?"

"Just now, when you talked to him. Any indication he'd been
drinking?"

"He kept sort of repeating himself, so I guess he'd had a few.
Don't forget, he was real worried about me. He thought I'd
been mugged or something."

Mugged. Olivia took a breath, tried to be matter-of-fact.
"I'm asking because of the father in *Perfectly Honest.* Didn't he
always start out with a couple of good belts, straight from the
bottle? To crank himself up for the tortures ahead?"

Lori's turn to stare speechless. Then, in a whisper, "What
are you saying?"

"The thought of you dealing with Rob tonight terrifies me.
Tomorrow morning's soon enough. At least by then you'll be
able to count on your own sobriety."

"That's heavy, Olivia. Incredibly heavy."

"Yes."

"But what do I *do*?" She sounded like a little kid forced to
follow rules no one had ever explained. "I can't just call back,
say I changed my mind."

"Of course you can. Especially since he doesn't know where
you are." Olivia was stopped by a thought. "Does he?"

"No. At least, I never said. At least I don't think so. But how
do I . . . What should I tell him?"

"As little as possible. You've had second thoughts, you need
some time, you'll call in the morning when you've thought
things through."

"You don't know him! He'll have a fit!"

Olivia reminded herself that even if Lori had let her where-
abouts slip, Rob couldn't break into a house that had resisted

burglars all these years. "Let him. You're out of reach. Safe. He starts to argue or yell, you tell him to stop or you're hanging up. He doesn't stop, you hang up."

"Wow. This is unreal. Totally. Okay, here I go. I'm actually going to do this. Now I'm walking over to the phone. Now I'm . . . I'm . . . totally about to lose it."

She dropped the receiver and sank heavily onto the sofa. "What I'd really like . . . Would you . . ." She broke off, gave an embarrassed laugh. "God, you really hit the nail on the head, I'm drunk as a skunk. Okay, I'm just gonna come right out and ask you. Olivia. Would you please sit with me? Right here close? In case this call changes my life or something?"

5

Olivia woke with a hangover. She hauled herself out of bed, pulled open the curtains, blinked at what looked like sullen cold. The walk to Mikey's, with plenty of deep breathing, might help her head. She dressed quickly in jeans, turtleneck, and sweater.

The door to Abbott's room was closed. No sound within or from the boys' bathroom; Lori must be still asleep. She crept downstairs, hugging the banister, trying to step where the old treads creaked least.

Outside Dee's door she heard the whistle of his kettle. Right on schedule despite his late night—she'd been up to pee around two and heard him coming in. Staying out on a school night wasn't like him. Reaction from his white-bread weekend, she supposed.

Once outdoors, it struck Olivia that her quiet on the stairs hadn't entirely been hostessy consideration for a sleeping guest. Rather, she hadn't wanted Lori to wake and discover herself free to wander the house unsupervised.

Never let a stranger in your house. The oft-repeated warning had been her mother's; hearing it now in her mother's exact voice, Olivia gave herself a shake. What horror, precisely, might Lori commit? Would she rummage through bureau drawers? Steal the silverware? Spit in the milk?

Olivia hated cautious, fussy people. People who elevated order, privacy, nice-and-clean, over warmth, kindness, comfort, hospitality. Who "set a lovely table," only to serve microwaved prefabs because real cooking made such a mess of the kitchen.

And why did she hate them so much? Because she knew, to her sorrow, that a nasty pocket of caution and fussiness lurked in her own soul. No matter how wholeheartedly she wanted to open her house and sympathies to Lori—or anyone else in need—her mother's child kept her well supplied with conflicting ideas.

Mikey's was quiet, no rumor du jour afloat. Olivia paid for her paper and, still headachy, decided to extend her walk.

She followed a familiar route. Downhill first, through the grungiest section of the north slope, effective antidote to Beacon Hill's theme-park aspects. (Talk about nice-and-clean!) Then left on West Cedar, which grew increasingly upscale as she walked south. Left again and back uphill on Pinckney, once a border-street mix of north- and south-slope sociologies but now fully gentrified. The trees were burnishing nicely, especially on the sunny side of the street.

And here came Dee on his bike, tearing downhill. He didn't spot her until she yelled. Braked hard, his theft-proof three-speed squealed and bucked.

"Great form, Dee. Did you see Lori Lutz this morning?"

He hadn't, so she told him about Rob.

His reaction, if you could call it that, was an impatient toss of his head. "That's all?" Olivia asked.

"Pretty much. I can't say I'm surprised."

He'd do this, Dee would. Without warning, he'd go all world-weary and burned out on you. He'd seen too much, you were to understand. He couldn't get worked up over every fresh demonstration that humankind was an evolutionary error.

This stance of his could be a real pain. Difficult not to take it personally, as a personal snub. "I told Lori she could stay as long as she wants. She'll expect you to know what's up, so don't pretend or anything. But I guess we shouldn't discuss it outside the house until she gives us a green light."

"Right. See you, okay? I'm running late."

She waved him off. That *okay* had been tentative, shaded with apology. A feeble-enough olive branch, but offered in the nick of time. Another snub and she might have told her dear old friend to go screw himself.

Feeling out on a limb—Dee acting like a stranger brought the house total to two—Olivia ducked into her office instead of going upstairs for breakfast as usual.

The office Braun hadn't been used in weeks. She blew off the dust, measured out coffee that was far past its prime. Then she tilted the venetian blinds on the street-level windows so she could see out, feel connected to the public life streaming past on foot, bicycle, Rollerblades. However much she reduced her workload, she knew she'd never dismantle this office. The rest of the house was imbued with family, the doings and feelings of her family self. Here, surrounded by pretty apple-green walls, an art deco rug loomed in Shanghai in the thirties, the chairs and lamps she'd bought long before Mission got hot and costly, she experienced a separate identity. Not better, not lesser than her family self, just separate from it.

She hadn't always enjoyed such blessed balance, of course. Nor had Philip. Early on, neither had imagined such surefootedness was possible. The boys had to grow older, their days and hearts increasingly claimed by school, before she could feel less overwhelmed by her responsibilities as their mother. And Chapman Interiors had to grow into a real business with substantial profits before Philip, cut some slack on his provider responsibilities, could summon the time and energy to be a genuinely involved father, not just a dutiful walk-on.

The milk in the little refrigerator was clotted solid, the coffee more stale than she'd expected. And not much in the paper. She paged quickly, slowing only for Ann Landers, the funnies, and an article she'd never have read if not for Boy Lyman's shelter. Ostensibly it was a NIMBY story, taking place in the small industrial city of Brockhurst, some thirty miles south of Boston. Factory closings and consequent unemployment had virtually emptied several Brockhurst neighborhoods, their boarded-up houses much assaulted by vandalism and arson. Two days before, the Commonwealth's announced plan to convert yet another foreclosed house into a facility for retarded adults had caused a near riot. Enough is enough, was the consensus of the angry public. "We're way past saturation with these elements," a woman was quoted as saying. "First they tell us nobody needs skilled labor anymore," said an unemployed man. "Then they say the only thing we're good for is minding mentals and retards."

Olivia thought about it. What made a factory shift, eight hours of noise, fumes, and predictable, repetitive tasks, better work than minding mentals and retards? She wished the reporter had asked more questions. "Have you, sir, had any experience in taking care of people like these? Under what conditions?"

But maybe hands-on experience, when it came to your choice of work, was neither here nor there. Look at Boy Lyman. On the strength of little besides Lori's novel, he'd convinced himself past doubt that caring for down-and-outs was the noblest work the world could possibly offer him.

Funny how closely Brockhurst's complaints about saturation mirrored those you could hear on the north slope. Olivia cut the article out, stuffed it into the thick file she kept on neighborhood issues.

She wished Dunbar would call. Useless to start planning where and how to use Val until Val had accepted the deal. On impulse, she went over to her bookshelves. A lengthy search— unlike Philip and Dee, she never alphabetized books—produced her paperback of *3 Hots & a Cot*. She opened it at random and read:

> Marilyn brought the motor-pool Ford to a stop as smoothly as the laboring engine would allow. She eased the gearshift into "park," then switched off the ignition. No sooner had the clattering wipers been silenced than heavy droplets of rain covered the entire windshield. Taking a firm grip on her bright-red umbrella, she let the car door swing wide open. Dirty, murky water lay in a deep puddle alongside the curb. Carefully stepping over it, she snapped the umbrella open and availed herself of its cheery protection. Quickly, with determined footsteps, she marched up the flagstone path to the house.

She remembered now that Lori had a maddening tendency to bulk up every insignificant action. Turning to the beginning of the book, she prepared to skim.

Marilyn, put in charge of a shelter program for the homeless in a city something like Brockhurst, had been hardened by political infighting and corruption. By page three, Olivia knew that her control-freak exterior hid a grape-soft heart. Authorial softness of heart defined the homeless people introduced: all were victims of bad luck or, at worst, bad judgment. Criminality was represented by Spike, on parole from thieving he'd never have been driven to had society not denied him honorable ways to feed and house his family. And how had Spike's wife and daughter repaid his sacrifice? They'd split, before he'd even gone to trial, never to be heard from again. His prison term had been harsh; his parole officer was a pig, the kind of civil servant whose example had made Marilyn what she was today.

Olivia had just reached the Sheetrock sequence Lori had used to urge flexibility on Boy Lyman when she heard water running. Her guest was taking a shower. It was after ten. Suddenly ravenous, Olivia decided to make omelets. And whip up a batch of cornbread.

Encountering the creator of Spike and Marilyn had its surreal aspects. Olivia found it very different from coming face-to-face with Dee immediately after reading one of his stories. Dee's characters could seem briefly more real than their creator. With Lori, even this pale and depleted Lori, the adjustment ran in the opposite direction. It seemed a marvel that she was flesh and blood, not a cardboard cutout.

Olivia was glad she'd left the book in her desk drawer. She wouldn't mention her morning's reading.

Lori's eyes were no less bloodshot and puffy than they'd been the night before. She seemed edgy, constantly combing the fingers of her good hand through her greasy hair. She turned down everything but coffee.

Olivia flipped the pan to fold her own omelet and slid it onto a heated plate. Sitting across from Lori, who'd taken the chair she always sat in herself, she filled two mugs, added milk to her own, and cut herself a generous square of cornbread. "Plenty here if you change your mind."

"Oh, God. You've gone to all this trouble and I can't even—"

"Cornbread's easy," Olivia interrupted. "And I was hungry."

"You bake for yourself? Just like that?"

"Often."

"Amazing."

"Not really. The amazing time was before the boys went

away to school. They'd help, Philip too, but all four of us spent our lives on a treadmill between here and the Stop and Shop. We got so sick of hauling stuff upstairs, we almost sprang for an elevator. Now, unless the boys are on vacation, I shop and cook only when I feel like it. Even when I have guests."

Lori's dawning smile showed she got the point. Encouraged, Olivia continued. "How do things look this morning?"

"When I first opened my eyes, strange place and all, I thought I was still on my tour. For a second there I felt wonderful—safe and happy. Then the truth hit. You didn't hear me crying? Really? Wow. No one ever heard me when we lived in the condo, either. At least no one ever said anything or called the cops."

"Chances are no one ever will hear, now that you're living in a house. Which ups the danger for you."

Lori nodded slowly. Then: "Last night, when you said I could stay here as long as I needed to? Did you really mean that?"

"Of course I meant it." Of course she had. And still did. And *you*, she told her mother's child, can get lost.

"The thing is, Rob's made a bazillion promises to get counseling, every one of them totally, *totally* worthless. He's never even called to schedule an initial appointment. I'm starting to think he never will. Not that people can't change. If I move out, he might get shocked into seeing someone who can help him. I mean, stranger things have happened, haven't they?"

Lori seemed innocent of any suspicion that Rob had a girlfriend. Last night Olivia had decided to leave that can of worms alone. The woman hardly needed more grief. Now, unsure of how to comment on Rob's capacity or willingness to change, she stuck to practicalities. "What about clothes? And your work? Would this morning be a good time to pick things up?"

Lori's answer was a look of terrible desolation, more tears.

Olivia reached for the Kleenex box. "Am I pressuring you?"

Lori blotted her face, blew her nose. "No, no. You're being great. It's the finality, I guess. Plus, my book—I've been stuck so long I'm scared to start again."

"But look how well you worked when you got home from the tour."

"That was one day out of months and months. This book's a killer. Don't ask me why, because I don't know. All I can say is I've been slogging away on it forever, just trying to pile up pages, get something, anything, down on paper. I haven't dared read over any of it. And I won't lie to you, in some weird way, Rob's helped. It's like this disaster between us is so huge the book's a minor side issue. Now what, though? Once I call it quits on Rob, I'm all alone with the rest. What if I read through those pages and there's nothing there?"

Olivia tried not to think about Marilyn's tedious transition from car to pathway. "I know those worries," she said. "I'll work all day on a design without stopping to review what I've done. Facing it the next morning can take real guts. Still, I think it's vital for you to have your work at hand."

"I've never been blocked in my life, you know. Not for a second. It just flows, fifteen, twenty pages a day. And I don't have to do much rewriting, either. Basically, my first draft is the finished book." She sighed heavily.

"How's this? We'll go right now, pick up your clothes and whatever you need for writing. When we get back here, I'll help you set up your work space on Abbott's desk. If you're not ready to write, you can go to a movie, watch the afternoon soaps, do whatever you want. You use a computer, right? How heavy is it?"

"Not. It's just a Mac. The printer's light, too. You'd do that for me? Walk right into the lion's den?"

"I don't think he'll roar too hard at me." Though he might try to find out if she'd reported his cheating.

"But he'll know you know about him. That he hits me and all. He'll be furious!"

"So far he's kept his abuse furtive. I doubt he'll all of a sudden want a witness. Besides, it's nothing to me if he's furious. No emotional hooks, right? He makes noise, works himself into a broth, so what?"

Lori's eyes rounded. "Wow. That's . . . amazing. Totally amazing."

Now or never, Olivia sensed. "Let's go," she said. "I keep the van in the Common garage."

"Van? What for?"

"Your stuff. Isn't that what we're talking about?"

A groan. "I was imagining stuffing some things in a pillowcase. But you're right. If I want him to understand the old way is over and done with, I've got to put my money where my mouth is. Oh, my God. Money."

Olivia waited.

"What am I going to do for money? Rob handles all that—the bills and everything. I don't have a clue how much is in the bank."

"Do you have a joint account?"

"I don't know. Rob does the checkbook. Oh, God. I think I'm in real trouble. And it's totally my own doing. I was trying to even things out."

"What things?"

"Rob's written one book to my three. My books, the first two, anyway, made a ton of money. His got great reviews and didn't sell enough to cover his advance. And as far as being blocked, Rob's never known anything but. He works all day to produce twenty *words*—and has to throw them away the next day because they're not good enough. It was breaking my heart to see him. Tearing me to pieces. Talent to burn and nothing but frustration to show for it. So I asked him to, you know, do the finances."

"Did that help?"

"Yes, except he'd started drinking more by then. Between fights, though, it was definitely better. 'Specially when he made money on a stock he'd picked all by himself. Those were wonderful times. I'd play it cool, but inside I was singing and dancing. It was like I'd, you know, *done* something for him. Given him this sense of accomplishment he couldn't find on his own."

Telling this, Lori shone with pride. She seemed blissfully unconscious of what was starting to look like the central inequality of her marriage: She gave without taking, Rob took without giving. Olivia hated to bring her down to earth. "Do you have an ATM card?"

"ATM? Oh, for those cash thingies, you mean. Rob has one."

"How about credit cards?"

"No. Rob thinks they're usury."

"How did you pay for your book-tour outfit?"

"Rob gave me a bunch of hundreds."

"What about day-to-day cash? For groceries and so forth?"

"I get it from Rob."

"Oy."

"Not good, huh."

"We'll see. Let's hit the bank first." Olivia had a terrible thought. "You do know which bank?"

Lori did. Not the exact name, but the location. "Fantastic," said Olivia. "I know the manager. Nice guy named Frank Simmons. I did some work for him and his wife—a room quite a bit like this one, matter of fact." And Frank was the soul of decency. Last year, needing money for Philip's nursing home, she'd consulted him on a second mortgage. Hold off awhile, he'd said, interest rates are about to drop again. "Okay," she announced. "Bank, then van, then your stuff. Ready?"

"Shouldn't I call first? So Rob knows we're coming?"

Instead of screaming, Olivia opened the coat closet, handed Lori her poncho. "You're simply taking your own property from your own house. I say we surprise him. Forewarned is forearmed."

"My wife loves your books," Frank Simmons told Lori. "She's reading one right now. And I guess you know, Olivia, how much we like our new room. Not so new anymore, but we still call it that."

This auspicious beginning was followed by the banker's quick comprehension of Lori's needs. But for all his willingness to help, the computer was adamant: from the bank's point of view, Lori didn't exist.

The screen was positioned so that visitors couldn't read it, but the facts were so simple it hardly mattered. "Your name isn't on your husband's checking account or any other," Simmons gently informed Lori. "That means any withdrawal of any funds will require his action and signature. That's really all I can tell you. In fact, I shouldn't even have confirmed the existence of his accounts. The law's very strict: We can release account information in only one instance—to next of kin in the event of death."

Lori sunk in speechless misery. Olivia asked the next question. "They bought a house last year. Do you hold the mortgage?"

"I can't tell you that, either. Oh, what the hell. There's nothing here about a mortgage. He must have gone elsewhere. Not unusual. People don't like all their eggs in one basket. Ms. Lutz? Can you remember a bank name? From the closing?"

"I didn't go. Rob said I didn't have to."

"Did you, uh, sign any papers?"

"No. Rob took care of everything."

So the mortgage was in Rob's name, too. Simmons exchanged a glance with Olivia. She stood. "Thanks for seeing us on such short notice, Frank."

Lori stood too, looking surprised that a meeting she'd found so inconclusive could be over.

"Any advice on our next move?" Olivia asked.

Simmons pursed his lips. "It's probably time for a lawyer. The best you can afford."

Sandbagged, Lori swayed. Olivia got an arm around her. "Fresh air," she prescribed, moving for the door. It was exactly like walking a drunk.

As they crossed into the Common, Lori halted, her features slack, stunned. "This whole thing is so . . ." She trailed off, let her head droop. "Maybe I should forget it. Go home and just . . . forget it."

"What's changed, Lori? The money? You can write more books, make more money. Unless you hit your head wrong the next time he shoves you."

"Did he *plan* this? Set me up for this kind of fall?" Her voice sank, dry as ashes.

She's asking me to save her, Olivia saw. To show her I think she's worth saving. If I don't, she'll go back to him. And the next time he spins out of control . . . "Let's grab that bench," she said. "We need to discuss lawyers."

6

Lori collapsed onto the bench. "If only I'd paid more attention," she began, then trailed off into numb silence.

Olivia steeled herself. Wishful regret, against the savage fact of Rob's financial machinations, was futile. The sooner this ugliness was in the hands of a pro, the better. For herself, too. A rescue mission takes a bad turn, you can't just bail out. Ever since Frank Simmons had said the magic word, she'd known why lawyers were invented—to protect us from the penalties of our impulses, the kindly ones no less than the wicked.

She spoke more directly than she'd yet dared. "Frank's absolutely right about a lawyer, Lori. Bad enough Rob's hurt you physically; this is a whole other level of punishment. You gave him control over your money because you felt sorry for him. He took that generosity and trust and twisted it to defraud you. He was cool, careful, patient, and heartless. This is hardball, Lori. Without solid legal support, you've had it. You might never see a nickel."

Lori's lips were pressed into a thin, resistant line.

"Well?" Olivia prodded.

"It's like Rob says, Olivia. Lawyers only complicate everything. That's how they make their money."

Rob says. Good Christ. "Do you use an agent?"

"Sure, Pia Rosato. She's tops. Why?"

"She works on percentages, right? Say she's negotiating price with the publisher, do you want her to give away the store? Of course not. You want complications. Same as in decorating. I'm a pro, I'm full of ideas, all sorts of gorgeous complications. Does that mean the client loses the right to say yes or no? 'Course not."

Lori mulled this.

"You took a real shock in the bank," Olivia went on. "You need time to get used to it, and you probably need to talk about feelings more than finances. But don't forget, as long as Rob's got your manuscript and notes for the new book, your main hope of getting back on track is in limbo."

Lori let out a wail of anguish.

Olivia tried one of Dee's favorite theories. "I'm not just talking about making money. You're a writer; you need to be writing. You need the physical act of it, same as an athlete needs workouts."

Finally, with great reluctance, Lori caved. Seizing the moment, Olivia ran to the public phones outside the subway station and made a quick call to Mary Jane Hughes, the only lawyer in Boston she could pop in on without an appointment.

"Mary Jane's not a divorce lawyer," Olivia then explained to Lori, "but she'll give you her short list of good ones. She's juggling her schedule for us. If we hurry, we can have a half hour."

Lori blinked. "What good's a half hour?"

"With Mary Jane? Plenty. You'll see."

Mary Jane's office was in the Little building, a short walk away. Olivia set off, just like Marilyn, with quick determined steps. Lori kept lagging behind. "Better pick it up," Olivia urged.

"Huh? Oh, sorry. I was just thinking . . . how do I pay for this?"

"Mary Jane's been counsel for Chapman Interiors from the

very beginning. She'll probably give us a break on the bill, and you'll pay me back when you can."

A reprise of last night's effusions, declarations of how wonderful, how kind and sweet, brought them the rest of the way.

Despite the longevity of their relationship, Olivia and Mary Jane were business, not personal, friends. The lawyer was proficient, humorless, indifferent both to popular culture and life's aesthetic possibilities. The brightest frump in town, Philip had called her. Today she wore one of her cheap drip-dries, navy blue and prim. Two white plastic barrettes from Woolworth's kept her straight brown hair out of her eyes. Her only jewelry was a rudimentary wedding band.

Expecting chic, Lori was thrown off balance by the utilitarian office and Mary Jane herself. Who, no surprise, had never heard of the famous best-seller or Rob's brief critical success. Learning that Rob had a lock on the finances, she went straight to the point. "Do you have any monies about to come in from royalties, reprint rights, film sales or options?"

Lori wasn't sure. "Rob keeps track of all that."

"Don't you endorse the checks?"

"Usually Rob does. He has power of attorney. Besides, he's the one who figures out what the checks are *for.*"

Lori's smile pleaded for understanding. Mary Jane sat stone-faced. "You and your husband share the same agent?"

"No, he has his own."

"Good."

You'd have to have known Mary Jane as long as Olivia had to detect the extent of her relief.

"In fact," Lori continued, "Rob's had fights with Pia. Real doozies."

"I suggest you call her immediately we finish here. You don't want any more checks mailed to him. Get a post box or use Olivia's address. And I suggest you cancel his power of attorney without delay. Let's move on to discovery issues."

Surgically interrupting whenever Lori strayed from fact to emotion, Mary Jane was ready to summarize in less than ten minutes. "One"—she folded down the pinky of her left hand—"you believe that your marriage is over and, fearing for your life, you are quitting your common domicile. Two"—down, ironically, went the finger with the rudimentary ring—"you intend to seek a divorce on the basis of extreme cruelty. Three"—the up-yours finger, too late: Lori had been thoroughly screwed already—"you will tell your agent to send all monies to you directly. Four"—index finger—"you believe your husband will resist giving you access to tax returns, canceled checks, or statements from banks, brokerage houses, and credit-card agencies. Five"—thumb down—"you are not a signatory to your home mortgage."

Mary Jane regarded the fist she'd made, turning it this way and that. She's evaluating its force, Olivia guessed. Knockout punch? Or only a body blow, brutal but survivable?

One further question: "What about insurance?"

Lori perked up. "We have it for people slipping on the front steps and all. Oh, and Blue Cross."

"I was thinking of life insurance."

"Oh. I don't know. God, you must think I'm a total moron."

Mary Jane shrugged. "You're not the first wife to ignore finances. Okay. You're moving out when?"

Lori looked at Olivia. "Now?"

Olivia nodded. "The idea was to take him by surprise."

"Just the two of you?"

"Actually . . ." Lori began.

Olivia made herself wait. Mary Jane just waited.

"I was just thinking," Lori hesitantly resumed, "maybe I should do it alone. Rob really hates it when people know his business."

"He'll have to adjust," said Mary Jane. "Divorce is a legal and public event, just like marriage. At any rate, you shouldn't be alone with him, now or at any future time. That will seriously undermine your assertion that you were obliged to move out because you feared for your physical safety. Further, it will open you to a countercharge of abandonment, in which case you could lose financially. So don't go in the house alone. On the other hand, Olivia, I'm not crazy about you sticking yourself in the line of fire."

"Oh, come *on*," protested Lori. "You're making Rob sound like some kind of homicidal *maniac*. I mean, it's broad daylight! Plus, he's not a morning person. Lately he's been real logy until way into the afternoon."

Olivia swallowed what bubbled up in her throat—wild laughter or an exasperated howl, she wasn't sure which.

"I like plenty of witnesses," Mary Jane said. "Dee's around, isn't he, Olivia?"

"Forget it." Lori was more decisive than she'd been all morning. "Bringing in a *gay*? Rob'll go ape for sure."

"Up to you," Mary Jane told Olivia. "At least leave the front door open. And don't mention what you learned at the bank. No point provoking him. Also, if you think he's been drinking or using, leave until you can bring reinforcements." She checked her crummy old Timex. "Now. Lawyers. You can expect to pay up to three hundred an hour."

"Wow. For how many hours?"

"You'll have to ask them individually."

She handed Lori a sheet of paper. "I can vouch for everyone on this list because I know them and their work personally. All of them are tough, intelligent, and willing to work hard. They're good diggers—you're going to need that, given this fiscal situation—and good negotiators. And not afraid to go to court if, God forbid, it comes to that. You should be prepared to shop carefully, because you and this person are going to be partners, maybe for a long haul. The chemistry has to be right."

"Shop? You mean, like, interview them? Won't that cost me?"

"Some attorneys bill the preliminary, some don't. You get into a long-haul situation, it's money well spent."

"The thing is, I'm totally broke."

"You don't know that." Mary Jane looked at her watch again. "I've got to run. Olivia? Can you hang around while Ms. Lutz calls her agent?"

"Sure," said Olivia, full of admiration at this inescapable shove toward fiscal fact.

And then, topping herself, Mary Jane thought to switch on the speakerphone. "Two heads are better than one," she said, but Olivia guessed her real reason. If Olivia could hear the agent firsthand, Lori couldn't mix up details, make a muddle out of nothing.

Pia Rosato was in; Lori introduced Olivia and managed to communicate the basics of her plight without falling to pieces. Then things got grim. Last week Pia had sent Rob a twenty-five-thousand-dollar check, the first of the "disappointing" paperback sale of *Sweet Harmony*. "As I explained to Rob, a hundred thou looks pretty low after the eight we got you for *3 Hots & a Cot*. But publishing's incredibly reactive, you know. Always looking back instead of forward. *Home Cooking* was a national best-seller and a major motion picture, whereas *3 Hots*—"

"Okay, okay," Lori interrupted, protective as always of the book so few had loved. "When will I see the rest of the *Sweet Harmony* paperback?"

"Next year, of course, once it's published."

"So what am I supposed to live on right now? How do I hire a lawyer?"

Silence in New York, then: "You wrote *Home Cooking*, you're bankable. I can get you an advance for the new book—what's it called again?"

"*Follow Me*. It's this slogan they have in the army."

"Right. I can get you a sight-unseen advance, but it's not

going to be what you need. Once I have your proposal and chapters in hand, everything changes."

"Okay. I hear you."

"I don't want to nag when you're going through a hard time personally. But it's months since you promised me those chapters, Lori. That's a long time to stay happily on hold, you know? Just tell me, can I expect something soon?"

Lori grimaced. "Soon. I've got to set up shop at Olivia's, all that."

"Fine. I'll let you get back to work, then. Take care, huh? And stay in touch."

"Wait. Could you, your agency, I guess I mean, sort of consider lending me some money? On account, sort of?"

"Well, like I told Rob last time we talked, things are crazy tight in this business. I'll speak to my partners, but I warn you, the accountant's watching every paper clip. Best thing, send me those chapters. You do that, we've got a whole new ball game."

Boston's one-way streets, baneful to drivers but the salvation of its residential neighborhoods, sent the van circling first the Common, then the State House. Near the archway where Olivia had encountered Rob and his girlfriend, Lori caught her breath, slid down in her seat. She'd spotted Boy Lyman. "I don't want him seeing me like this."

"Coast's clear," Olivia said when Boy was behind them.

"Why do I even care?" Lori then cried. "You're totally destroyed by your own husband, it's going to show."

"You look fine," Olivia soothed. Spotting a parking space just three doors beyond the house, she backed neatly in and gave Lori a matey cuff. "Good omen, huh? Maybe it's telling us Rob's gone out."

Lori shook her head. "He never goes out this early. God, I feel so *sick*. Throw-up sick. I'm afraid I'll do something crazy in there."

"You'll be fine. You've got justice on your side. He's the brute, not you. And I'll be right there for you."

Olivia had stuck a box of heavy-duty garbage bags in her tote. She now gave these to Lori. The plan was for Lori to pack while Olivia kept Rob diverted with talk. Lori would bring down the first load, a light one, then stay on the front steps with the door open, ready to give alarm if Rob should interfere with Olivia's removal of the remainder.

The houses along here had small front yards, roughly twenty feet square, a considerable luxury in a district so densely built. Most yards were carefully planted and tended, some enclosed by wrought-iron fencing, massively antique. The Lutz/Mallory setback, a litter-strewn jungle of overgrown rhododendron, yew, and rambunctious ivy, must annoy the neighbors, Olivia thought. Enough to deafen them to cries of pain in the night? Could people be that petty?

Lori, visibly trembling, had to use both hands to steady the key. "Should I ring the bell?"

"Of course not! It's more your house than his."

The foyer had a bare bulb dangling where a fixture had been. The living room was sparsely furnished in new-looking Roche Bobois, much cluttered by newspapers, magazines, and dirty glasses. "He's probably in his office," she whispered, pointing at the ceiling. "My stuff's on the third floor, so we can't avoid . . . Could you sort of . . ." She spiraled a fluttering hand upward.

"Lead the way? Sure."

A huge orange tiger cat padded out, gave them the once-over. "Bingo," Lori whispered. "Don't pat him, he bites."

Even though they'd left the street door open, Olivia had to fight images of movie staircases with menacing shadows, an ominous sound track. Her pounding heart seemed louder than her footsteps. Surely Rob could hear.

And there, movielike, he appeared, on the topmost step. The batterer. In the flesh.

"So *that's* where she's been," he murmured. He might have been filling in the last squares of a particularly humdrum crossword.

He obliged the women to squeeze past him, Olivia the filling of the marital sandwich. In the hall they regrouped, Rob lounging against the doorframe of his study, Lori sidling hesitantly toward the next flight of stairs, Olivia keeping protectively between.

Lori didn't speak until she was beyond range of his fists, and then was barely audible. "I'm picking up my work. I'll be staying with Olivia for a while."

"Just your work?" Rob's tone was one of friendly concern. "Won't you want clothes? Your lovely new wrinkle creams? Fat pills? Diaphragm?"

Lori gasped, turned as if to hump her back against a rain of blows, fled upward.

Diaphragm? Olivia wondered. After Rob's glorifications of vasectomy?

She could hear Lori crying, but her job was to stay here, isolate Rob from the packing process.

She regarded him dispassionately, imagining him as an item in a shop window. A small, badly-built bureau trying to pass for antique. Mismatched knobs, one certain to fall off at first tug.

"Shall we?" Rob said, sauntering toward his desk. "She's *not* efficient, our Lori. Might as well wait in comfort."

He sat, gave his swivel chair a playful whirl. The screen of his monitor was lit but blank. The room was strikingly neat, orderly stacks of magazines on the lower shelves that covered three walls, books ranging above. No dust. Rob, too, looked spruce in a flannel shirt and corduroys, though he hadn't yet shaved.

Olivia took the room's other chair, a capacious number covered in soft black leather. The seat felt warm, a creepy but useful clue to what Rob had been doing when interrupted. On the lamp table lay a battered paperback, Paul Bowles's *The Shelter-*

ing Sky. There was also a hefty, new-looking biography of the Marquis de Sade, facedown and opened near the middle. Terrific. Rob had spent a busy morning researching his favorite indoor sport.

"Like that chair?" he asked.

"It's very comfortable."

"Birthday present from doting Lori. More accurately, a replacement. The chair she picked out on her own was vastly more expensive and altogether hideous."

Think bureau, Olivia reminded herself. Banal, charmless, absurdly overpriced.

"You're censorious, Olivia. Let me guess. Have the two of you been splashing in the mud puddles of wifely complaint?"

Don't provoke. "No."

"Bullshit. Never mind, I can fill in the details myself. Our Lori is incapable of advancing past the basic plotline that has served her so doughtily these many long years. Big hairy male oppressor, poor dear little female victim. Isn't her enthusiasm for these size imbalances strange? When you consider that she and I are roughly of a height? Of a weight, too, most of the time. Gosh, I hope she doesn't forget her fat pills."

That did it for Olivia. "Why does the wife of a man with a vasectomy need a diaphragm?"

He laughed, less to cover his surprise than to relish it. "Ah. A woman who remembers things. Why indeed? Roadwork? You'll have to ask her. Perhaps the next time you girls have another natter about my friend Kim."

"I haven't mentioned Kim, matter of fact. Probably I won't. A woman with her writing arm in a sling hardly needs extra grief."

Rob sighed. "Why do I hear blame? Surely you've observed that our Lori is clumsy. Her coordination is bad—ever see her try to dance?—and her peripheral vision is limited. A fatal combination. She's constantly plowing into doors, tripping over the cat. You'd think she'd learn, but no. She wants to change a lightbulb, she picks the most rickety chair in the house. It's her desk chair, actually; ponder the symbolism if you want a treat. Thing shivers if you so much as rest an eye on it. You don't believe me? Go up and see for yourself."

"I've seen enough. Her jaw, for instance."

Amused: "What's this? When?"

"Right before the book tour."

"You *have* been swallowing it. The big hairy male oppressor responsible for *that* outrage was Barry Linderman, DDS." Rob gave the phone a push in her direction. "Call and ask him."

Ice water ran down Olivia's spine. This little bureau had trick drawers, secret compartments. But Lori might have secrets too. No ordinary woman could have faked the anguish that had poured from her last night, but writers of fiction are not ordinary. As Dee was fond of saying, "They lie for a living. They steal without conscience. Everything you are, everything you say, is theirs for the taking. They'll snatch your soul right out of your breathing body."

Was this couple, then, a matched set? The question had no sooner surfaced when Olivia squelched it. Rob's financial defrauding of Lori was incontrovertible, appallingly concrete. Nothing Rob had insinuated about Lori today came anywhere near it in scale, malice, or impact. Besides, she'd signed on only to protect, not to judge. Leave all that to the lawyers, the divorce court.

Her moment of doubt over, Olivia gave the phone, and Rob's invitation to use it, a dismissive wave. On the stairs, footsteps; soon after, Lori stood at the door.

Her face was smudged as if she'd wiped her tears with a dusty hand, but the task of packing seemed to have calmed her. "I'm done," she told Olivia. "It's a lot—four big bags plus my Mac and the printer."

"Fine. Wait downstairs, and I'll get started."

Rob leaned back in his chair, taking his ease, hands clasped behind his head. The batterer as amused onlooker.

On her way upstairs Olivia passed, at the end of the hall, an immaculate bedroom dominated by a king-sized bed. A lofty down comforter in a dark-green duvet served as spread, pillows cased in plain white were piled against a Shaker-style headboard. There was a single table, with none of the usual bedside clutter, and one reading lamp. Was only one person allowed to read in bed? If so, Olivia would bet anything that this privilege was Rob's. The top of the simple, functional bureau was bare. No pile of pocket change, not even a comb or hairbrush. A green scatter rug lay by the lamp table; the rest of the conspicuously dustless floor was uncovered. There were no pictures, no mirror, no chairs. Aside from the luxurious bed, an anchorite's cell.

The floor above was unmistakably Lori's territory, strongly redolent of what Olivia, to her consternation, now knew to be Lori's personal odor. There was a study and a bedroom, just as below. Though Olivia had worked for a number of couples who wanted separate bedrooms, this, separate floors, was a new one. The case could be made, she supposed, that the setup had been dictated by Lori's and Rob's radically different housekeeping standards. Lori's bedroom made the living room seem tidy by comparison. A huge overstuffed chair sprouted its innards. There was a large new television set, a small old radio, quantities of scattered magazines, several pizza boxes. The narrow bed was a tangle of dingy sheets and frayed, stained blankets. Did Rob, in a mood for slumming, ever visit this bed? Or was sex restricted to the orderly lair below, Lori allowed in only after she'd scrubbed herself from head to toe?

In her study, more squalor. Ancient posters of Carole King and Carly Simon—romantic ballads; figures—were taped to the walls along with an array of greeting cards, postcards, and snapshots. Most of the snapshots were of Rob. Thick dust lay everywhere. Pulled up to Lori's computer was a kitchen chair as rickety as Rob had described. The mugs, glasses, and crockery that had been brought up here and forgotten would fill a kitchen cabinet. Dregs and moldy crusts intensified the sour smell.

Computer first, Olivia decided. Rob watched as she passed but said nothing.

On Olivia's final trip down, Rob, who'd resumed his post at the door of his office, broke his silence. "So now you know."

"Know what?"

"Why I need a decorator. Not to mention an elevator."

Olivia risked clearing up a point. "I thought of asking Dee to lend a hand here, but Lori said you'd freak out."

His face tightened. "I don't *freak out*. Over sodomites or anyone else. But you remind me of something I've often wondered. Were he and your husband ever an item?"

Bureau, Olivia thought, hoping her disdain showed. She started down the stairs.

Rob darted for the banister. "Lori? Can you hear me?"

Don't answer, Olivia silently willed her. But, good as gold, Lori bit. "Yes, Rob? *Yes?*"

"How many novelists of your undistinguished ilk does it take to change a lightbulb?"

The look on her face wrenched Olivia's heart. She'd obviously been hoping for some words of farewell.

"Give up?" said Rob. "Okay. It takes two. One to insert the bulb, the other to provide that boring old twist at the end."

Lori fell to pieces. By the time Olivia managed to bundle her into the van, faces had appeared at several windows. Neighbors, wondering what in the world was causing such commotion.

7

Wheeling out his bike the next morning, Dee looked ready to conspire. "How's it going up there?"

"She's upset because Rob hasn't called," said Olivia.

"But you two are getting along like a house afire?"

She shrugged. "It's a shakedown cruise. Can't expect smooth sailing with new crew aboard."

"Shoulders to the wheel, you swabs! What's with the nautical clichés?"

"Dunno, Dee. You're the wordsmith."

"They're macho clichés, come to think. Which is curious, because Joy Street's talking sisterly solidarity."

Olivia gave him her sweetest smile.

"In general," he went on, "we fall back on clichés to evade precise consideration of our actions or feelings."

"Isn't that interesting," said Olivia.

"Isn't it," said Dee, and went off to work.

Had there been a shakedown period when Dee moved in? Olivia couldn't remember. Different circumstances, of course—the cataclysmic upheaval of Philip's accident, the fact that Dee was a time-tested friend, not a neighborhood ac-

quaintance. Also, she and Dee were early risers, Lori a determined night owl.

And Dee didn't smell.

It was day two. Olivia was finishing lunch, Lori breakfast. Lori
had given a detailed account of her attempt that morning to
wash her hair. She'd no sooner gotten the plastic shampoo bottle open, using her teeth, than it fell from her good hand,
bounced, and the shampoo started running down the drain.
Trying for a speedy retrieval, she had slipped and banged her
sprained wrist hurtfully against the tiles.

"Let's not do that again," said Olivia. "How about a shampoo at that place you like on Newbury Street? My treat."

Lori gave her greasy curls a quick rake with her good hand.
"Oh, God, I couldn't. I mean, it's really *really* nice of you to
offer, but I just can't face them. They'll ask me stuff and I'll be
all . . . you know."

"Someplace new, then. Where no one knows you. Because
don't you always feel better with clean hair?

A shy smile. "What if . . . could we do it right here? Use the
spray gizmo on the kitchen sink?"

"Get your towel," said Olivia. "And my shampoo if yours is
all gone."

A wonder she could speak, so strong was her gag reflex. Lori
gone from the room, Olivia shook her head in disgust. What
kind of woman gags over the simple prospect of washing another's hair?

And what kind of woman, hours afterward, can't shake the
eerie vulnerability of a bowed neck, a ghostly white, water-
drenched scalp? Creepy, Olivia pronounced, trying to blow it
off. But the shadowed truth pestered: This was creepy with a
sexual edge. Olivia had been around long enough to take the
weirder promptings of sex in stride—nursing an infant, what
an interesting surprise *that* had been—but necks and scalps?

She'd never yet lusted after a woman, and Lori seemed an

unlikely point of departure. When all was said and done, did the two of them have enough in common to really *like* each other? Ah, but sex, she reminded herself, is about power, too. Lori's submissive posture, the delicacy of her neck bones, might have stirred some primitive, hidden murk.

Hidden for good reason. Watch Oprah, read the morning news.

These disturbing ideas led to a question. Had Rob and Lori started out quite playfully, Lori exploring vulnerability, Rob dominance? Consenting adults, as they say; who's to judge what people do in their own bedrooms?

There'd been nothing playful about the scenes Olivia had witnessed from her window, Lori on Rob's choke chain. Perhaps this period marked the beginning of Rob's rogue turn. But had Lori, turnabout, gone rogue herself? Gone ever more abjectly submissive because Rob liked it? Because arousing his interest was worth any risk?

Deep waters. Too deep for Olivia. And the shampoo hadn't banished the sour smell seeping from Abbott's room.

Taking pains, she made a meat-loaf-and-baked-yam dinner.

"*So* good," sighed Lori, taking seconds.

"My kids love it too." Olivia might never again get such an opening. Breezily: "Speaking of which, they pack for vacation just the way you had to, sweaty athletic gear jammed in with clean stuff. I have them put everything through the washer, and probably you should, too."

Lori set down her fork. "It's bad, huh?"

More breezily still: "Nah. I'm just cursed with a sensitive snoot. You'll be humoring me."

Lori's head drooped. Get the ax, she might as well be saying, finish me off. "Rob's sensitive too. He says I stink like a mink."

"Lori? Don't mix me up with Rob, okay? Because he and I are not alike. Not remotely."

"Was I mixing you up? Really? Wow. Wonder why."

Deep waters. Olivia murmured something and the dreadful moment passed. Or seemed to.

Normally Olivia would run to Dee, ace decipherer of human murk. Not now. It would feel disloyal, a betrayal both of hospitality and her own best intentions. Besides, Dee seemed interested only in complaining.

"She was pacing again," he reported the third morning of shakedown. "She went out about ten—"

"I know. It worries me, her wandering around at night. She says she's always done it. Helps her sleep."

"Sleep! She *paces*, I tell you. At one in the morning!"

Dee's bedroom was right under Abbott's; never before had he mentioned noise. "Hard to believe a grown woman makes more noise than a teenager," Olivia mildly observed.

"Abbott's *normal*. At one in the morning, he's asleep."

"Look on the bright side," Olivia said. "If she's up and about, she must be writing."

Dee groaned. The evening before, he'd been trying to finish his cleaning chores. Lori had trapped him on the stairs, gone into excruciating detail on the dire necessity of bashing out enough chapters, one-handed, to secure a contract for *Follow Me*.

"Come for supper tonight," Olivia invited. "I'm making paella."

"Can't. Papers to grade."

Olivia knew he'd say no. Lori's arrival had staved a waterline hole in their easy sociability. Reduced them to ships passing in the night.

Next morning: "She settled on a lawyer yet?"

"No. Listen, Dee, is it really such a great big deal having her here? She needs shelter and moral support. I'd say the house has room for her. In both senses."

"Fine. Terrific. But look how open-ended things are. She's broke, can't move into a place of her own. So how do you ever get rid of her?"

"That's borrowed trouble. It hasn't even been a week yet."

"Really? Seems longer."

"Huh," said Olivia by way of giving this a pass. There'd been times when it had seemed longer to her, too, but she'd never tell. Sworn silences were getting thick on the ground. She wouldn't ask Lori whether her dentist or Rob had given her that swollen jaw. And, Lori never mentioning her diaphragm, Olivia wouldn't either.

"Too bad she's such a slugabed," Dee now mused. "Otherwise you could have breakfast together too, instead of just lunch and dinner."

Olivia pretended this wasn't bristling with poisoned darts. "Mm. Except it's nice I can count on having the morning to myself. By midday, I'm ready for company."

"Wonderful," said Dee.

He's jealous, Olivia realized to her astonishment. All this carping is nothing but jealousy.

Not that jealousy was nothing. "Anyway," she backpedaled, "she's not around that much. If she's not scouting lawyers, she's over at Boy Lyman's. Big neighborhood meeting tonight, in case you hadn't heard. He's presenting his plans for Lyman House, as it's now officially designated. You going? No? Huh. I wouldn't miss it for the world."

Dee smacked his forehead. "Of course! Lori Lutz—God, I've been so *blind*—is only the thin end of the wedge. Inspired by her *powerful* novel and the *sublime* charity of Boy Lyman, you, too, will convert your house to an SRO. Fantastic! Historic Beacon Hill offers the poor pathetic homeless not one but *two* facilities. Break out your handkerchiefs, honeys, we got strong men weeping!"

Olivia sought help from heaven above.

"Oh, but silly me," Dee rattled on. "I clean forgot! Who's more vulnerable to homelessness than *moi*? The original at-risk kid! Dare I hope your new facility will spare a tiny corner? For an old retainer?"

"Dee," she protested, but he'd gone slamming out the door.

She was furious with him. His dependence on her for housing was an issue they'd resolved long ago—or so Olivia had believed. To bring it up like this, in jealous anger, demeaned both of them.

Besides, friends—true friends—*support* what you're trying to do. They don't sit on the sidelines and snipe at you.

Dee and jealousy. An old story, really. From college days.

He and Philip had been at Yale, she their weekend visitor from RISD, Rhode Island School of Design. And just as Philip's friendship with Dee had encouraged her to look past Philip's rather starchy surface, his conventionality, her presence allowed the two men, one openly gay, one unambiguously straight, to draw closer.

Almost instantly they'd become comrades, three friends who liked to play together. No sex. Olivia had an artist boyfriend in Providence, Dee his circle of gay friends. Philip, healing from a painful breakup with a Smithie, was resolutely celibate.

Made in heaven, made to last, so perfectly reciprocal and harmonious was their trio that when she and Philip fell into bed for the first time, astonishment nearly eclipsed lust. Discovering himself betrayed, Dee went on a long, lacerating bender, wouldn't speak to either of them for weeks.

That, she now decided, had been excusable jealousy. But to slip your moorings over the likes of Lori Lutz—

A ring on her office line. Dee, ready to apologize?

But it was only Steven Dunbar, saying, with endless backing and filling, that his girlfriend was unhappy with the deal Olivia had offered. "Basically I gotta sympathize," he said. "Val's an artist. She needs her freedom of inspiration, right?"

Olivia made the kind of face her mother always said might freeze and then she'd be sorry. "You're saying you want her to take over, finish the job?"

"What? Oh, God no. She'll just be handling the, you know, the colors. The walls and other stuff she wants to faux."

"But didn't I make that clear? You and I have already settled the color scheme. I've placed orders and you've signed contracts. Upholstery hammers are tapping as we speak. If Val wants changes at this point, it's going to cost lots of time and money. And if she *doesn't* want changes, then we're back at square one: she should agree to work under my direction so you won't end up with a *fritto misto*."

"Say again?"

"A mixed fried. A jumble. A mishmash."

"All I know is, she doesn't feel she can work under you. For artistic reasons, of course. Nothing personal."

"Of course not. And of course she, and you, will understand that for my own artistic reasons I don't want to leave my name on a mishmash. I'll bill you for services to date and that will be that. If you want, I'll attempt some damage control on the contracts, but no guarantees. You'd best be prepared to pay twice for everything Val won't use. Including those tiles you wanted for the guest bathroom. They're almost finished, by the way. And gorgeous. Beyond our wildest dreams."

"Jesus, Olivia. You're really putting it to me, you know?"

"Nothing personal."

"Yeah."

Women, she heard. If he'd said it aloud, she'd have slammed down the phone without another word. Instead, she told him to let the thing hang for a day, sleep on it, call with his final decision first thing tomorrow morning. "Right, sure," he said, and they hung up.

"*Men,*" she shrieked. Any louder, she'd have cracked the paint on the walls.

* * *

Lori's central preoccupation, Rob's failure to call or come hammering on the front door, was briefly overtaken by a new question. What should she, board member of Lyman House and but-for-the-grace-of-Olivia homeless woman, wear to tonight's informational meeting?

"Jeans for me," announced Olivia. The performance of civic duty, in her opinion, suspended the commandment that a decorator look unfailingly snappy. They—the Green-up Committee, Clean-up Committee, Lyman House; she didn't distinguish—were lucky she'd show up. They didn't deserve panty hose too.

"Yeah, except your jeans and my jeans . . ." Lori grimaced. "I guess it's back to the book-tour look. Fresh from the cleaners, thanks to you. I'll use the scarf for a sling. God, do you think Rob will come? He hates things like this, but . . ."

The prospect of encountering him seemed at once to frighten and excite her. "Don't worry," Olivia soothed. "You'll be among friends."

The meeting was held in the grand salon. Since Olivia's tour, someone had been at work, replacing defunct lightbulbs and chasing cobwebs. Instead of mice and mildew, there was a trace of Murphy's Oil Soap in the air. The carbolic of the gentry, Philip used to call it.

And instead of spooky silence, a buzz of excited chatter. The good turnout had filled every one of Boy's new folding chairs except at the very front. "Just like school," Lori said as she and Olivia took places there. "No one wants to be near the teacher. Oh, great, Boy got the floor plans enlarged."

Mounted on posterboard and propped on easels, the plans flanked a small table that held glasses and a pitcher of water. The way these meetings usually ran, Olivia knew there'd be plenty of time to stare at plans later; she turned to see who'd shown up.

Her good friends Nanda West and Drew Lispenard waved

from three rows back. Kristen Jacobs and several other north-slope neighbors waved too—people Olivia had worked with in favor of trees and window boxes and against the lavalike encroachment of neighboring institutions: Mass. General, Suffolk University, and the government of the Commonwealth, eternally hungering after new office space, brazen sneak thieves of the citizenry's parking slots.

Good souls, Olivia's neighbors, with civic energy to burn. You could predict where they'd come down on dog poop and elderly housing, but an SRO for the homeless? Impossible to say.

She saw Peter Robertson, the man who'd complained of Boy's stubbornness. No sign of Rob.

"Hi, Olivia."

It was Michelle Greene, stylish in a wine-red chenille tunic that set off her pale, fine-textured skin. Indoor skin that made Olivia feel craggy and weatherbeaten, like Clint Eastwood.

"I've been meaning to call you all day," Michelle went on. "Let's chat after this, okay?"

Olivia said fine, and Michelle made for a chair near an easel.

Lori was grinning like a fool.

"Did you engineer that?" Olivia asked.

"No! She was wondering where to find an interior designer willing to donate some time. I mentioned you lived close by and she lit up like Christmas morning. Are you mad? Should I have warned you?"

"Not at all," said Olivia, "surprises are nice. And it's always nice to be asked."

But was she, in fact, ready to sign on? The voluntary aspect fit right in with her new freedom to concentrate on making a life, not simply a living. Also, now that she'd been asked, she had no trouble admitting she'd love working with a star like Michelle. But what about working with Boy Lyman?

Here he came, stoop-shouldered and haphazard as ever, settling himself at the table, pouring a glass of water, spilling some on the dog-eared pages of what looked like a long speech. In his wake arrived the rest of his directors: Charlie Pierson, Becky Krebs, and Helen Rowantree. Pierson and Rowantree, active proponents of several north-slope conversions, were not only south-slopers but residents of Chestnut Street. Lower Chestnut, to be sure, blocks from Boy's house, but at least they'd stuck to their principles. Pierson had the added clout of Grand Old Man–hood. Nearly eighty, he was still square-shouldered and springy. Krebs lived at a remove from north-south factionalism, in the riverfront area known as the Flat of the Hill. (A true Bostonian, Olivia knew, would find nothing hilarious in this designation, but she wasn't a true Bostonian.) Krebs was an excellent choice. She had founded, and for many years managed, Children's Corner, a widely admired day-care center.

Boy stood and cleared his throat, his expression doleful. Several in the audience made shushing sounds, but nothing silenced the charged-up din until Helen Rowantree, six feet of dignified patrician authority, beat on Boy's water glass with the blade of her Swiss Army knife.

"I want to welcome you and thank you for coming," Boy began.

"Can't hear," cried voices all over the room.

Lori strained forward, as if to will Boy all the strength and conviction she could muster. His anxiously darting eyes found hers and locked.

Pure blue electricity. Olivia blinked, startled by its force, its visibility. Lori, too, was startling. Olivia hadn't seen this side of her since the morning of Boy's house tour.

When Boy repeated his welcome, everyone heard just fine. He introduced the board and Michelle Greene, seeming to gain confidence with each name. And when he launched into his talk, he did so without reference to the pages piled before him.

"There's been a lot of speculation about my intentions," he

said, "no end of rumors flying around. Tonight I'd like to start with what the board and I hope to achieve at Lyman House. Then we'll answer your questions, as fully as we can at this preliminary stage. The floor plans are preliminary, too, but Michelle Greene is ready to share with you her basic concept.

"I hope everyone understands that this property's current status is a rooming house. Licensed as such, even though it hasn't been used as such for some years. The alterations of floor plan Michelle will show you are toward the goal of offering housing, and, crucially, counsel and moral support, to ten single men and women now homeless, as well as up to eight homeless families.

"Originally I wanted to set up a very basic shelter, first come, first served, similar to the shelter in Lori Lutz's wonderful book, *3 Hots & a Cot*. But after long consultation with Lori and other experts, including the wonderful Beacon Hill neighbors who agreed to serve on our board, I now believe our true challenge and primary effort should be toward breaking the cycle of poverty that contributes to homelessness. Lyman House will not be a stopgap, Band-Aid, or revolving door. By pulling talent from our neighborhood as well as the Boston area's many colleges and universities, we will help our guests use their time with us to gain the tools for a vocation and independent living.

"We are fortunate in that we will be privately funded. Frankly, we don't think that existing city or state programs have much to teach Lyman House. They seem to stop at what is, rather than aspiring to what can be. We aim to do better. Much better.

"Now, some of you might say we're a drop in the bucket, the homeless problem's too huge for little individual efforts like ours to make a dent. But I promise you, friends and neighbors, we intend to succeed. And we expect our success to spread, to become a model for others, many others, to follow.

"I've talked enough. It's your turn."

Silence. The audience wasn't ready. Either they'd been led astray by the thick wad of pages, or no one wanted to be the first to fling ice water on Boy's lovely dream.

"Will there be an increase in density?" a familiar voice finally asked. Way to go, Kristen, thought Olivia. Density worries, in jam-packed Beacon Hill, were unassailable. Right up there with motherhood and apple pie.

"We're currently licensed for twenty," Boy said. "Our plan, as I said, is for eight single rooms on the fourth floor. The third and second floors— Michelle? Could you flip to— Thanks. You can see there are a total of six two-bedroom units. Each unit could house two adults and one child, or, more likely, a single parent and up to two children. So, yes, we'll be petitioning for an increase of numerical density up to a maximum of twenty-six. That's six children, remember. We feel it's vital to serve families as well as single people."

Some back-and-forth followed, simple questions, for the most part, briefly answered. Why not have only families? Should the single rooms be evenly apportioned between men and women? Why, when there were so many more homeless men than women? Will residents have to go through a screening process? Who'll screen them?

Next, bricks and mortar. What about food facilities? Michelle again worked the easels, showing sweeping changes in the basement level. "I trust you will restore this magnificent old room and the conservatory," said an elderly man. "It would be criminal to allow further deterioration."

"What would be *criminal*," a much younger woman riposted, "is to waste money on nineteenth-century excess when twentieth-century children need computers."

"Recent studies have shown," a man declaimed from the middle of the room, "that providing free shelter to these unfortunates simply allows them extra money to spend on booze and drugs. It's your basic law of unintended consequences."

Lori turned in alarm to Olivia. "Who's that?"

"Bud Morrison," Olivia said. "He has a recent study for every occasion."

Charlie Pierson was on his feet. "I'd like to speak to that, Bud. We've seen those studies too. They're not entirely without merit. That's why Lyman House will be a supportive *residence*, not merely a physical shelter for the night. By the same token, we have neither the desire nor the capability to serve as a drug-treatment center. We will not accept guests who use illegal drugs. Period. If someone begins using them, he or she will be told to pack up and leave."

Morrison wasn't finished. "What about booze? Smashed bottles on the sidewalk. And vomit."

Pierson sighed. "Our government, in its wisdom, has deemed alcohol a legal substance. We, too, will treat it differently from other drugs. As Boy indicated earlier, Lyman House will work closely with a variety of counselors and community organizations, Alcoholics Anonymous very definitely included."

Pierce sat down and Helen Rowantree stood. "I'd like to add something. Lyman House communicates something terribly important to the disadvantaged of our society. You belong here, it says. You, no less than any other American, deserve to enjoy this beauty and tranquillity and historic preservation. *You are worthy*, Lyman House says. Now, that is a *very* powerful message. Once its full meaning is absorbed by a formerly homeless individual, his or her self-esteem will improve dramatically."

Morrison again, archly skeptical: "You have any studies on that, Helen?"

A luminous smile. "No, but I have proof. Looking around this room, I see people with good strong senses of self-respect. And guess what, Bud? They also respect their environment. And that's why our streets and sidewalks are so clean and tidy."

She smiled again and sat down to the night's first applause.

Not rousing. Rather perfunctory, though augmented by several heartfelt cries of "Hear! Hear!"

Olivia turned to catch the reaction of her friends in the third row. Nanda gave her a droll wink. Drew rolled his eyes.

Olivia smiled to say that she, too, thought the self-congratulation was getting awfully deep.

"I think the facility per se is a fantastic idea," declared a newly elected member of the Beacon Hill Civic Association, an earnest young man whose name Olivia could never remember. "But I do question its appropriateness for Beacon Hill. What about selling this property and putting what would certainly be a very substantial gain into a facility that's better sited? In a more appropriate part of the city?"

"Don't discount Beacon Hill on appropriateness," Boy smartly returned. "Lyman House is close to two general hospitals and two major psychiatric centers with innovative and effective outpatient programs. An easy walk in any direction leads you to all sorts of entry-level employment opportunities—retail, hotels, fast-food outlets. We're surrounded by free educational and recreational opportunities, including the Public Library, Boston Common, the Public Garden, and, not free but a real bargain, the Charles River Sailing Pavilion. Bowditch is a seafaring name, you know, and I hope to see a fund endowed for just this precise use. Above all, we can offer daily contact with the values of hardworking, successful people like yourselves—a priceless and unique opportunity to learn by example."

"Am I the only skeptic here tonight?" drawled a voice from the last row.

Rob. Lori went rigid.

"Can I possibly be alone in questioning this marvelously uncritical endorsement of our so-called community's so-called values? I look around the south slope and what do I see? A half dozen or more households that have profited enormously from the S and L debacle. A prominent banker linked with the red-lining that virtually destroyed black Boston's housing base. A plethora of lawyers who spend their days turning bankruptcies, divorces, and personal-injury cases into all-you-can-eat buffets. And let's not forget our developers, whose shameful indifference to aesthetics and greedy abuse of the public weal is sustained and enabled by still more lawyers."

He paused to let his charges sink in. From the audience, no coughing or fidgeting, just frozen, appalled silence. Some, Olivia thought, must be praying he wouldn't name names.

"Perhaps mine is a minority view," he then continued, his tone more conversational. "But to foist the values of, say, an S and L profiteer on a group of unwary indigents strikes me as not only mischievous but the height of presumption."

As before, Boy sought Lori's eyes, Lori's strength. And came up empty. Lori was a goner.

Becky Krebs leaped into the breach. "I happen to believe in the American dream, and I'm not afraid to say so. No sensible person would claim that Beacon Hill is the Garden of Eden. All Lyman House wants to say is that living on a clean, tree-shaded street, among comfortable houses in good repair, among people who tend to business and their kids' education . . . All we're trying to say is, sure, life can never be more than what you, personally, put into it . . . what you struggle to make of it, but . . ."

Seeing her flounder past recovery, Rowantree rose to take over. "Doesn't an orderly and predictable environment make life easier for everyone? Regardless of his or her station in life? Surely we can all agree to that."

"Golly," breathed Rob. "Any minute someone's going to remind us that Mussolini made the trains run on time."

Scattered laughter, some nervous, some dangerously joyful. Rowantree showed her exasperation but wouldn't be snubbed. "I'm curious, sir. Why did you yourself choose to live here?"

"I like the architecture."

"Can we take it, then, that you'd willingly expose—what was your phrase?—unwary indigents to this architecture?"

"Sure."

More uneasy laughter. Boy made a manful grab at leadership, gesturing toward a woman who'd had her hand in the air for some time. "You've been very patient, ma'am."

"I just wanted to say one thing. Beacon Hill is predominately white. Many of the homeless, the ones I see, anyway, downtown mostly, are people of color. Would they be comfortable here? Because Chestnut Street . . . I've never actually known a person of color to live on Chestnut Street."

"Me neither," said Boy. "But so what? Newcomers feel comfortable when the people who got there first want them to feel comfortable. So stay with your thought, okay? You've put your finger right on how an idea like Lyman House impacts us. How it confronts us with our hardest questions and most worthwhile questions. Like, who are we? What do we really believe in? What kind of society do we want for ourselves and our children?"

Not bad, Olivia decided. Not bad at all. Rather than arguing with Rob, he'd taken up his sneering comments, and moved them toward real inquiry.

"We've strayed pretty far for the first night," Boy continued. "Let's adjourn for now, meet again in a couple of weeks."

Objections—"We're just warming up!"—seemed overwhelmed by expressions of endorsement and relief.

"The ayes have it," Charlie Pierson declared, conviction making up for his absence of orthodoxy.

As was usual with civic meetings, the audience dispersed slowly, supporters and critics alike gathering around the various people who'd spoken up. Olivia was interested to notice that no one approached Rob. He gave them plenty of opportunity, wrapping his scarf slowly around his neck, gloving himself as deliberately as a stripper in reverse motion. But no one came. Had he made himself too toxic, even for the people who'd laughed at his Mussolini crack?

Olivia had almost laughed herself. Helen Rowantree's old-money serenity could be mighty irritating.

Rob caught her watching him, broke into a life's-a-hoot grin. Then, no rush, he strolled out of the room.

Lori's relief was obvious. She and Boy had been standing side by side, meeting their public with fixed, strained smiles, braced for Rob's next strike. They'd kept their cool, though. Boy especially.

Had Boy acquitted himself sufficiently for her to sign on, cheerfully call him leader? Oh, why not. Life's a hoot.

Michelle was at the easels, penned in by the usual noisy contingent of wannabe designers and architects. Olivia pushed her way through, touched her arm.

"Olivia! I'll be a while here. Can you wait?"

"Let's talk first thing tomorrow."

"Eight too early? Fine. Just tell me—yes or no?"

Olivia answered her smile. "Yes."

"Fabulous." She turned back to the wannabes. "You heard it here first, folks. Whatever else, Lyman House is going to have colors to die for."

Smiling with what she hoped looked like modest pleasure, Olivia made her way to her friends Drew and Nanda. "Let's go drink," she said.

"Our house," said Nanda. "You haven't seen Caroline in ages, and she's never cuter than when she's asleep."

"I warn you," said Drew, "this meeting has put me in an Alice Roosevelt Longworth mood. She had a sofa pillow that said, 'If you can't say anything good about someone, sit right here by me.'"

Olivia laughed. "Thank God for true friends." Oh, but wait. She had to tell Lori she wasn't coming straight home. And— shit!—she had to tell her in a way that didn't prompt her to come along, join the fun.

Foolish worry. Lori and Boy had made their own plans for the rest of the evening. Yet another intriguing morsel to gossip over with Drew and Nanda, feet up, hair down, problems at the crest of Joy far, far away.

8

Michelle Greene called on the dot of eight; the exchange that followed made Olivia glad she'd said yes last night.

"Lori's husband's a corker," Michelle said at one point. "Those negative role models sure gave the crowd something to chew on."

"In the nick of time," said Olivia. "I get nervous when the rich start in on what the poor should learn from them."

"Yes, but I liked it when Boy said the residents could teach us a thing or two. About what we believe in, what kind of society we want."

"I hope he's right. My own theories always crash into a brick wall of economic reality. Materialism's evil, I proclaim. It mires people in envy, greed, and covetousness, three of the Seven Deadly Sins. Four, if you count gluttony. But if people don't buy, buy, buy, the economy crashes, taking the good stuff down with it. Since I love parks, museums, great music, I have to love malls, too."

"And since we love Lyman House," Michelle asked, "we have to love the triangle trade?"

"At least. Don't forget the S and L types and the rest of Rob's rogue list we'll be hitting up for contributions. Who was the designer on this job, anyway?"

"This . . . ? Oh, I get it. Modern society, you mean." Michelle laughed. "Here's a silver lining: It probably wasn't a woman."

What would Dee make of her involvement? Olivia wondered when she and Michelle had hung up. Not that she cared, the way he'd banged out yesterday, not a word since.

The phone again. "Oh, hi, Steven," she said.

"Yeah. *That* Steven."

Cross. Something in her voice had tipped him he wasn't uppermost in her mind. "You've made your decision?"

"What's been *made* here is a royal pain-in-the-ass mess. Val's not talking to me. No surprise to you, right? Oh, come on. Who gave the ultimatum?"

Olivia remembered to take a deep breath, repeat her question.

Still cross. "How can I decide anything when she won't even take my calls?"

Trusting to the watertight perfection of Mary Jane's contracts which left the client, not the decorator, with all financial liability, Olivia offered him an extra day.

A pause as if he, too, were taking a deep breath. "I'm crazy in love, that's the bitch of it. She's got me wrapped around her little finger, and all I can do is pant like a puppy and beg her to marry me."

"For heaven's sake, Steven. This is wedding bells? Well, why didn't you say so in the first place? No wonder she's throwing her weight around—she wants to build what's going to be her own nest. Perfectly natural inclination. Anything else, you'd have to worry she wasn't going to stick. Let her take over. With my blessing, and yours too. It'll cost, but what're you saving it for?"

"That's really okay with you?"

"Yup. Actually, I can use the slack. Michelle Greene's signed me up for a project here on the Hill."

"*The* Michelle Greene? Hey. Big time, Olivia."

"Tell Val. If she knows I hobnob with the famous, maybe she'll smile on our tiles."

Dee came in for his bike. "I was a jerk. I'm sorry."

"Me too." Olivia didn't care if he took that both ways.

"It's all this change and confusion. No knack for it."

If he was referring to Philip's death, he could say so plainly. She was in no mood to draw him out. "Lori's short-term," she said. "You're not."

"I know. You aren't either. How was the meeting?"

Making no mention of Michelle, Olivia sketched the rest, concluding with Rob's diatribe.

Dee grinned. "I have to admit, he's got a point."

"Mm," said Olivia, their truce too recent for more.

Lori stumbled sleepy-eyed into the end of Olivia's lunch. "Boy's *so* long-winded," she said, yawning. "He kept me talking all hours."

"He sure does think the world of you," said Olivia.

Lori laughed. "Tell me about it. God. I mean, he's *not* my type. Poor thing—Rob really got to him."

"Rob got to a lot of people."

"Yeah. He's a powerhouse. That's what I woke up with this morning—Rob's incredible power and how it relates to my writing. Writing's his be-all and end-all, so it had to be mine, too. He refused to take time to make friends, have a life, so I did too. And now I'm like, okay, subtract Rob, what's left? Do I still want to write? And if I do, why? Exciting questions, huh?"

"Very," said Olivia. She could see it all. Lori, bridges burned, penniless, permanently installed. At the Thanksgiving table, around the Christmas tree, on the ski slopes at spring break . . . "What about the writing you've done since you got here?" she thought to ask. "It's not satisfying to you?"

A half-smile, evasive. "It's hard. I'm totally conditioned to typing two-handed."

"Sounds like this isn't the best time to decide what writing means to you. You've got what, another week in the splint?" Olivia tried not to sound as if she'd been counting the days. The shampoos.

"Eight days until my checkup appointment. But with this pain I'm having, I'm not that optimistic."

"What are you taking for it?"

"I've got to deal with that today, actually. 'Oh, please, Mr. Doctor, *please* refill my Percocet. I don't want it for the high, really, truly, I don't.' " She gave a short laugh. "How can they call themselves healers? Make you grovel for a decent night's sleep."

The phone rang. "That you, Lori?"

Olivia said just a minute and covered the mouthpiece. "A man," she said. "Not Rob."

The caller did most of the talking.

"You're positive?" Lori asked at length. "Okay. I might need to get back to you." She hung up very deliberately. "Rob paid cash for the house," she explained in a flat, dry voice. "He owns it free and clear." A harsh sob, then: "If he can show he built up the capital by his own efforts, trading stock and all, a judge could say I shouldn't even get half. How can this be happening to me? You know? I've basically given up hearing anything good from Rob, but how much more bad is there gonna be?"

"I'm so sorry, Lori. Was that your lawyer?"

"What? No. Just this guy. Friend of a friend from my waitress days."

"How's the lawyer search going? I'd expected you to ask me for some money by now. You're not holding back, are you?"

"No. No one's charged me yet." The evasive smile again. "Two of them said they liked my books."

89

"Nice. How were they otherwise?"

"Okay, but they were both women. I think a man's better for standing up to Rob, but the men I've seen . . . We just don't click, you know?"

Near dusk that cold, blowy afternoon, Olivia was in her office. The floor plans Michelle had sent over were spread around, the door closed against drafts. She heard the street door opening, leather heels percussive on the marble floor of the little foyer. Hadn't Lori gone out in her usual Birkenstocks? Yes, there they were, padding along with the aggressive heels. Stifled giggles, then nothing but two pairs of feet climbing the stairs.

Another stranger? Surprised and annoyed—and annoyed with herself for being so testy and territorial—Olivia decided to give them five minutes.

A weirdo, was Olivia's first thought, Lori's brought home a weirdo. The two women were seated opposite each other at the dining table, leaning urgently over their elbows, profiles close.

Lori greeted her, the soul of happy hospitality. "Meet Felicity, Olivia, Felicity Starshine. Isn't that a fabulous name? She's just been mugged—right by Filene's. Can you stand it?"

On a plate in front of Felicity were ice cubes, a wad of reddened tissue. The right side of her face, badly scraped, was still bleeding.

Olivia sat at the head of the table. "That must hurt."

Felicity shrugged. "Fucker bounced me pretty hard, but I'd've won except the strap busted. It was a shoulder bag—I had it on crosswise."

"It's awful, Olivia," said Lori. "She lost a whole weekend's work and five hundred dollars."

"No cops around?"

Felicity looked disgusted. "Kidding?"

"I was there right at the end," said Lori. "Not that I"—a disparaging flick at her splint—"could help much. He was a big guy, young. Jeans and those huge sneakers. Sweatshirt with the hood up, so I could hardly see his face. Just enough to know he was African-American."

Felicity snorted. "When the cops finally showed they asked could I do a positive ID. I had to laugh. 'What's to pick?' I said, 'these yos all look alike.' "

Felicity delicately slid an ice cube over her scrape, then, wincing, blotted with fresh tissue. "You want to call that racist, be my guest," she invited Olivia. "I basically avoid eye contact with men, period. Black, white, yellow, red, I don't discriminate. Saves hassle."

"Men *do* look alike," said Lori. "At this party a couple of years ago? In one of those special Beacon Hill gardens? Every man had on gray pants and a navy-blue blazer. Every single one. Finally even they had to notice it. And you know what? It really set them up. Like it was this major confirmation or something."

"Pathetic," said Felicity.

She's a species of skinhead, Olivia decided. Her eyes, dark and large to begin with, were magnified by shaved eyebrows, fake lashes out to here, sooty shadow, and eyeliner. She wore street-mode basic black: tights, a baggy tunic sweater with a deep cowl, Doc Martens boots. A leather biker jacket with lots of silver zippers hung on the chair beside her. She was older than she had first seemed, her skin crosshatched, almost as if veiled, with tiny wrinkles. Fifty, Olivia thought, maybe more. Was it gutsy of her to have fought the mugger? Stupid? Her dark hair, cropped like a Roman centurion's, was frosted by metallic gray.

The kettle whistled. Lori jumped up. "I was making tea, Olivia. If that's okay?"

Felicity grew intent, as if hoping Olivia would snarl, No, it's *not* okay. "I'd love tea," she said, breezy, breezy. And then, while Lori clumsily set out the cups: "You lost a weekend's work, Felicity? What kind of work?"

"I had six, seven rolls of film in that bag—color film I had to drop at the lab. Don't get me started on how my own darkroom got ripped off. And *don't* say what the cops said, that the bag might turn up minus the cash. Losing that film is a total and unmitigated disaster. So don't be asking me to conjure a lot of *hope*."

"I won't," Olivia promised.

"I mean, we're not talking *spigots*. This is core creativity. You can't just switch it on and off *at will*. Workshops are serendipity, synergy, unique moments in time. And don't forget, for most of my women it was a major first, exposing their secret selves. Yo Fuckhead takes it into his head to develop that film, their deepest fantasies will be hung out in public. How are they supposed to live with that?"

"It's bad," said Olivia. "I'm really sorry."

"Why?" Felicity demanded. "It's not your fault."

"Sorry it *happened*," Lori hastened to explain. "Like, sorry for your trouble."

Felicity shrugged. "I'll live."

Lori tried another idea. "You know what I think? I think it's really important to call up the women and reconvene the workshop. As close to now as you possibly can. Once they commit to something in the here and now, they'll be less freaked about what's over and done with. There were what, six of them? Would it be that hard to round up six women for another go?"

Felicity flipped an irritated hand. "You're not getting it. Basically what I do, I pry open windows my women slammed shut a long, long time ago—for their own personal and excellent reasons. And what's my biggest ally? Newness. The lure and rapture of the unexplored, untraveled *new*. I don't kid myself I can change you in a weekend, doesn't matter how productive the sessions get. This is where the photographs come in. Unlike ordinary facilitators, I can send my women on their way with *evidence*. Later, in privacy and at their leisure, they can study concrete images of the work we accomplished. 'Yeah, that's me all right,' they can say, 'I really did that, I felt those feelings.' Absent concrete feedback, all bets are off. They'll have taken terrible risks, laid themselves bare, and for what? Zero if they're lucky, worse than zero if the prints get out."

"But shouldn't you at least *try*?" cried Lori. "Instead of just leaving them to worry what some nameless faceless creep will do?"

Olivia had to ask. "Is there a lot of nudity?"

"A lot?" Felicity was deadpan, clinical. "Depends how you define it."

"Oh, my God!" said Lori. "All this yakking, Olivia, and you don't even know what Felicity *does*. It's so interesting! Tell her, Felicity."

Felicity was glad to. "I call it visactualization. Each woman uses her opposing archetypes as springboards. You're probably familiar with the whore/madonna dichotomy, but that's only the tip of the iceberg. Every workshop turns up new ones. Belle/bimbo, vamp/virgin. Virgin comes in a lot—virago/virgin, victim/virgin. And Mom. Mom/mischiefmaker, that was a terrific one. Slut/sorceress, angel/anarchist—the options are endless. Okay. How it goes is, society keeps women locked into the middle ground between these archetypes. Society says your opposing poles, call them black and white, are dangerous, and your only safety is in the gray middle. Which is a sure recipe for a boring life. As long as we deny the validity of our archetypal extremes, including their dynamic and inevitable opposition, we can never truly own our core selves. You following this okay?"

"So far," said Olivia. For herself, belle/bimbo? Or mom/mischiefmaker? She was torn.

"The workshop begins at the level of conscious speech. Articulation proceeds in diads, then triads, then encompasses the full group. Next we incorporate games, singing, various mental and physical exercises. Visactualization's ultimate goal is, one, to define the fundamental essence of our personal archetypes, and two, to dramatize them for the camera. I use lots of props—food, beverages, costume elements, slides of everything from great art to pornography. Basically anything that will prime the pump is grist for the mill."

"Sounds like a busy weekend." Olivia was carefully neutral.

Felicity, grave, nodded. "It's incredibly intense. The synergy is fantastic. And of course it's a sleepover. We bring sleeping bags. Amazing things happen when my women go into slumber-party mode."

"I bet."

"The workshops offer a safe, totally supported, nontoxic environment. I don't even have to advertise anymore, it's all word of mouth. I've actually considered quitting my day job. And now that shithead's fucked everything."

Nothing to say, they finished their tea in gloomy silence. Outside it was pitch-dark. Getting on for suppertime. There were two chops in the refrigerator. As far as Olivia was concerned, neither one had Felicity's name on it.

By way of compromise, she lifted the teapot invitingly. "No, thanks," said Lori.

"Where do I pee?" said Felicity.

Olivia pointed to the corner opposite the kitchen, where a tiny lavatory was concealed behind a curving wall of antique paneling. Felicity rose gingerly. "Oooch. Stiff as a board tomorrow. Hey. How do I get in?"

She was hardly the first person unable to find the cunningly concealed door. Olivia hastened to help.

"She's great, isn't she?" Lori then whispered. "I'd love to do a workshop with her."

"The larder's pretty bare," Olivia whispered back. "I'm going to ease her on her way, okay?"

"Sure. I'm sorry if I—"

"No, no. Sister in distress. I'd have done the same myself."
Baloney. You'd have run like a bunny. "Sh. Here she comes."

"It's like ice in there," Felicity complained. "Freeze your
ass."

"But isn't it neat?" Lori asked. "Like a secret chamber. And
see how the curve of the wall goes with the kitchen counter?"

Felicity regarded the two arcs but was not moved to comment.

Olivia made a mental note: Time to start leaving the door
ajar. Remodeling, intent on her complementary shapes, she'd
forgotten the tiny room would need its own radiator. She and
Philip had run an electric heater in there until bill one from
Boston Edison unplugged it forever. A pity to lose the secret-
chamber fun for five months of the year, but it did keep a key
lesson constantly reinforced in the decorator's mind: Comfort
first, design second.

Felicity was a master staller. Easing her home to Jamaica Plain
took time and tact. "Look," Olivia finally had to say, "I don't
like the idea of you hopping on the T with a head injury. If my
van were outside, I'd drive you home, but it's in the garage.
Blocks from here, and it's dark and cold—hear that wind? So
will you let me buy you a cab? For my own peace of mind?"

Felicity gave up with one of her shrugs. "You're that anxious
to throw money around," she said, "be my guest."

9

The following Friday, Olivia abandoned Lori to the menu options of the freezer and hurried downhill to dinner at Vahan and Kitty Kasarjians'. She was late. Lori, having spent the last few hours aimlessly moping, had confessed, last minute, ignorance of the microwave. And then revealed herself a remarkably slow learner.

Exactly the kind of stunt Ryland would pull. With her son, Olivia might manage maturity—"Scramble yourself some eggs, Ry, I'll give you a lesson tomorrow"—or lash out—"Absolutely not! You should've asked earlier!"

Why then, instead of making herself late, hadn't she been normally mature or normally snappish with Lori? Because she suspected that Lori's moping, ostensibly over Rob's silence, was really home-alone blues. She'd wanted to go to the Kasarjians', and Olivia hadn't even offered to wangle an invitation for her.

Shakedown, she told herself, let it go. You're having a night out in fabled Louisburg Square. The food will be yummy. And the surroundings? Michelle's appraisal would serve: "That dining room you did for the Kasarjians is one of the three or four most beautiful rooms in Boston."

Would people talk about Lyman House tonight? And in what terms? It depended, Olivia supposed, on how much the Kasarjians' appetite for social climbing had influenced their guest list.

Entering a room you've created, seeing it used as intended, always brings fresh satisfactions. The table, fashioned by Olivia's woodworker from long-hoarded walnut, would sit eighteen, and tonight they were twelve. Even so, the atmosphere was intimate, cozy. Recessed lighting subtly washed walls the color of aged brick. Simple pilasters of distressed fruitwood disguised the functional steel posts that made the room possible—formerly it had been the town house's basement kitchen and utility rooms. A heating grid underfoot banished clamminess; the deep-blue floor tiles were overlaid by a Caucasian carpet, a subtle geometry of muted reds and blues. Vahan, looking forward to long, animated dinners, had insisted that only Knoll's best desk chairs would be comfortable enough; they'd been covered in leather dyed a funky thirties green. The room's entire rear wall had been knocked down, the pilasters there framing tall windows and French doors. Beyond was a carefully planted and illuminated garden.

Olivia found her place card. Hovering at her right was Mr. Recent Studies himself, Bud Morrison. When she'd greeted him earlier, at cocktails, Olivia had had two hopes: that they'd be seated far apart, and that he wouldn't take her on about her new job. One down, one to go. She made sociable noises, wondering whether Morrison and his dull, pedigreed ilk would ever be invited anywhere if not for social climbers.

"Isn't this nice," he said, rolling out her chair, paying courtly heed while she settled herself. "Unusual, office chairs. Wouldn't have thought of them myself. How are those boys of yours? Good, good. One's at Cheshire, right? Terrific school, Cheshire. Top-notch. I wanted my boy to go there, but he was worried about the workload."

Olivia had heard him make this point before. It neatly exemplified their lack of common ground, Ryland having picked Cheshire because it was the least demanding school Philip had been willing to pay for. As before, she backed off with a murmur, a false smile.

Morrison's attention was quickly snagged by the conversation across the table. John Rawls was doing most of the talking. A central-casting Yankee—lantern jaw, keen blue eyes, silver hair—his subject was the latest frolic of some irrepressible scamp Olivia didn't know, even by reputation. She swiveled around—in a rational world all dining rooms would have these chairs—to see what Kitty had given her to cope with on the left.

"James Warriner," said this man, smiling.

Of course. Earlier, spotting him in the center of a knot of avid talkers, she'd been sure she'd seen him before, and now she knew where—in Mikey's store. Paying for her own paper, Olivia had noticed Mikey's *Herald* open to the "Separated at Birth" feature. The first photo was the famous one of John F. Kennedy at the tiller, tanned and merry, big square teeth as white as the sail of his Wianno Senior. The dead ringer was James Warriner, Suffolk County's new district attorney, appointed last month by the governor to fill out a term. Same teeth, same thick windblown hair, same rugged good looks.

"Those two really could be twins," Olivia had said.

"I heard father and son," said Mikey. "Which figures. A swordsman of Kennedy's caliber, he's bound to've knocked up a few."

Sudden silence among the ranks. Today's rumor, Olivia knew, had just been born.

Warriner, in person, resembled JFK less, Olivia thought. His features were sharper and more—what? Republican? Democrats, incensed that a Republican had been slipped into a Democratic fiefdom, had called his appointment "unadulterated cronyism" on the part of the governor. Warriner, they'd complained to the press and TV cameras, lacked "hands-on experience in dealing with the criminal element."

She smiled back at him. "Olivia Chapman."

"I know. Kitty told me you did all this. It's wonderful."

"Thanks. Clients like the Kasarjians make your work easy."

"What makes a good client? Money? These paintings are the real thing, yes? Who did the coast o' Maine landscape?"

"Fairfield Porter. The portrait's a Mary Cassatt. But money's not everything. Do you like this wall color?"

He looked around, considered.

A good sign, Olivia thought. Too many people, invited to look, would do anything but.

"I do," he said. "Very much."

"These walls were sponged and glazed, but you could approximate the color for only pennies more than using plain white."

"I hate to tell you how much plain white I've slopped around here and there. I go into the store and see those hundreds of colors they have, you know, those racks, and grab for the white. In desperation. Does that make me a bad client?"

"Potentially, but not inevitably."

He threw back his head and laughed. And was instantly more JFK than he'd been thus far. More sexy, Olivia guessed she meant. Kitty saw, too, and caught Olivia's eye. Gave her a look that meant Go for it, girl.

Blushing, Olivia dived deeper into the ostensible subject. "Desperation turns some clients panicky. They shut down and won't tolerate anything besides beige, vanilla, tasteful little prints. Kitty and Vahan aren't like that. When we first talked they'd just been to a major Matisse retrospective. Great rich blooms of pattern and color—and a quality of light, not to say life, that's nothing like Boston's. So, much as I love color, I had to rein them in."

"Or what?"

"Or garish. Like the stuff you buy in hot-climate markets.

You unpack at home and the magic's gone. That's never happened to you?"

"Not yet. My ex-wife's idea of travel was Stowe in winter, Mount Desert in summer. But"—he dropped his voice and waved an encompassing hand—"what about this for garish?"

Kitty had never met a Deruta pattern she didn't like. The table was, as usual, set with a wild profusion. Sometimes her combinations worked, tonight they didn't. But before Olivia could respond, Bud Morrison leaned across to interrupt.

"Jamie? We need an expert opinion on this homeless shelter Boy Lyman's ramming down our throats. He's saying there'll be classes in this and that. I say classes are what you have in a school. Beacon Hill code says no new schools in residential areas."

"That's right," said Kitty. "They shut down a woman's cooking classes, right here on Louisburg Square. Which I happen to think was incredibly stuffy. What's so dreadful about cooking?"

"It's the principle of the thing," said Morrison.

"Read Kant," Rawls concurred. "Act in accord with what you would wish to see as universal practice."

Kitty smiled and dropped it. Deference to the men? To social climbing? Whichever, Olivia, having seen that charming smile in other contexts, knew her heart was elsewhere.

"Code or no code," said Willa Keaton, on Rawls's left, "this thing smells like a done deal. I'm sure you'll agree, Jamie, that City Hall is absolutely delighted. Finally, after all these years, a chance to get even."

"Get even for what?" Warriner asked. Keeping it light, Olivia noted, without seeming to slight the importance of a voter's opinion.

"For the way we've ignored them."

"By *we* you mean . . . ?"

"The pols, of course. We don't vote for them, we don't beg them for handouts or jobs for our brothers-in-law. We take care *of* ourselves *by* ourselves, and it drives them wild. It wouldn't surprise me a bit if one of those darling Irish fellows put this horrid little bug in Boy Lyman's horrid little ear."

"Sad case, Boy," agreed John Rawls from across the table. "Never been able to make his mark in the real world. A shame, really. Awfully hard on his family."

"Well, I hope you don't think he's free to make his mark at *my* expense, Johnny. I have no intention of living next to a bunch of bums, crazies, and drug addicts. I'll lie down in front of the bulldozers if I have to. And I won't be alone, either."

"There won't be bulldozers, Willa," Kitty soothed. "Not in the historic district. Besides, I heard it was for families."

"Families?" Willa had to laugh. "I've read those bleeding-heart stories the *Globe* keeps pushing. Susie Q. has seven children, each one by a different man, no fathers in sight. Not quite what I'd call a *family.* Oh, and why is this woman homeless? Because she, or her latest boyfriend, take your pick, spent the rent money on drugs and she got evicted. Boo-hoo. Poor Susie Q."

"Poor children," said Olivia. Not that she herself hadn't weighed in, plenty of times, on the subject of feckless breeding. But this echo, punctuated by the flash of diamonds on Willa Keaton's pampered hands, turned her stomach.

"Poor children exactly," said Kitty. "I blame the Catholic church. All this agitation against birth control and abortion, and then the minute the baby's born, it's, Sorry, kiddo, you're on your own."

Rawls frowned. "Unfortunately, Kitty, it's not just the Catholics. Your fundamentalist Protestant sects are tireless in these arenas."

Morrison's full attention was on Olivia. "I just remembered, you're the one who took in Lori Lutz. Terrible thing, a man who can't control his temper. I never liked him, you know. He's a smart aleck. Embarrassed himself at that meeting, didn't he?"

"Lori Lutz?" asked Willa. "The writer? My daughter adores her. Utter, *utter* trash, but at least it gets her away from those horrible music videos. What's she got to do with Boy?"

"She's on his board," Morrison said. "Feeling as strongly as you do, Willa, I'm surprised I didn't see you at the meeting. They sent personal invitations to all the abutters—or so they told me."

"Gordon?" called Willa, her husband being deep in conversation with Vahan at the other end of the table. "Yoo-hoo, Gordon. Did we get invited to hear about this ridiculous shelter?"

"What ridiculous shelter?" asked Gordon.

Willa rolled her eyes. "The one that's going to destroy our life. Boy Lyman's fiasco. You know."

Gordon, clearly, did not know. "I put a bunch of stuff on your desk."

Silly woman, he'd practically said. Willa looked daggers. Not a happy marriage, thought Olivia.

"Who else," Willa then demanded of Morrison, "has Boy lured onto this so-called board?"

Morrison told her.

"Good *lord*," breathed Willa, stunned. It was far worse than she'd thought.

"Actually," said Warriner, "he asked me."

A bombshell. Kitty, as hostess, jumped in. "For heaven's sake. And you said no?"

"Had to. I'd just gotten my summons from the governor and I didn't think I'd have the time."

Willa's eyes narrowed. "Otherwise you'd have said yes?"

"Your fathers," said Rawls to Warriner in a tone of discovery, "were great friends."

Warriner smiled at the older man. "Still are. But that's not the only reason I'd have said yes. No, wait, hear me out. Social-service entitlements are really socking it to the city's working people, especially blue-collar families. We've got to find new ways to give them some tax relief. Approached with that premise, Boy's residence is just plain good sense. The private sector stepping in where—"

"I tell you," interrupted Morrison, "this is a *school*. Like they say, if it looks like a duck and quacks like a duck and walks like a—"

"I heard he's actually been asking the neighbors for *money*," cried Willa. "He certainly won't see a penny from me. Nor, I trust, from anyone who calls me friend."

Rawls pursed his lips. "The basic idea, insofar as I understand it, is not without merit. I do question its appropriateness for Chestnut Street."

Not without merit. Were these guys, at birth, issued a phrase book? "Where would it be appropriate?" Olivia blandly inquired.

"Oh, I don't know. The South End, I suppose. Or some other mixed-income area."

Warriner, of all people, jumped on this one. "Are you saying you don't think issues like homelessness and poverty are Beacon Hill's concern?"

"No, no, of course not. I'm a small-*d* democrat and a small-*c* christian. I believe in the community of mankind. If we don't hang together, we'll all hang separately."

"Oh, that's so true," cried Kitty, the Kitty Olivia liked best but hadn't seen much of tonight. "It's *vital* that we help one another. Before Vahan came riding up on his white charger, I was trying to make it as an actress in New York. Hand-to-mouth, always scrounging for rent and groceries. I had to have a tooth pulled because the pain was driving me crazy, and I couldn't possibly swing a root canal. Right on top of that there was a fire in my building and there I was, out on the street with nothing but the clothes on my back. I was lucky because I had friends, good friends who let me bunk in for weeks on end. If not for them, I honestly don't know what I'd have done. It's the kind of experience that leaves a mark."

They sat dumbstruck. Kitty was their hostess. Her skillful and attentive staff had labored to fill their bellies with splendid, rich food, was making their heads giddy with pourings of rare and glorious wines. Her artless confession and its inflammatory implications—No one can be safe! No one is exempt!—compelled response, but what?

"Ah, youth," someone finally sighed.

"The power of the artistic drive!" exclaimed another.

The platitudinous chorus swelled. How brave of you, Kitty, how *dedicated*, how really *very* interesting, until adroit Warriner had the presence of mind to change the subject.

"Jamie or James?" asked Olivia. He was walking her home. Trash day tomorrow, the sidewalk impassable for two, they'd taken to the street.

"James, please."

Olivia snickered. "Jamie's just for Republicans?"

"It's one of those great divisions of humanity. Some love baby names, some don't. My great-grandmother, substantial in every other respect, was Mousie until she died—at ninety-six."

"My husband's parents insisted on Pip for Philip. He hated it."

"Kitty told me about him. I'm very sorry."

"Thanks." There was something familiar about the couple coming toward them. When the gaslight showed their faces, Olivia grabbed James's arm. "Trouble coming," she whispered. "Don't talk."

"Well, well," Rob crowed in delight. "The decorator and the DA." He turned to his friend. "What d'you think, Babes? Does he really look like JFK?"

"Hi, Rob," said Olivia, tugging at James to pick up the pace.

Kim put her mouth to Rob's ear, said something that made him yelp with joyous laughter. "Who's *JFK*? God, what a broad. What a *broad*. Fucking national treasure, that's what you are, Babes."

"Charmer," James said when they'd gotten clear.

"He's marginally worse unstoned."

Sketching her link to Rob and Lori brought them to the crest of Joy. Someone nearby was having a noisy party. Olivia looked upward, saw lights in every window but Abbott's.

"I'll say good night," she said. "Lori was moping about being stuck at home, and who knows where her head is now. By the way, I've never mentioned Rob's girlfriend to her, so the less said on that, the better."

"Sure. Well. Let's get together soon, okay? What's better for you, lunch or dinner?"

Olivia hadn't had a date since falling in love with Philip, but the code hadn't changed. Lunch was lite, dinner not. "Either's fine," she dodged.

"I'll call." A wide smile offered with his card. "Or you call me."

"Whichever happens first," Olivia promised, putting her key in the lock. If he'd been older than she instead of the other way around, she'd have picked dinner in a flash. Stupid, but there it was.

From the open door, a burst of cheering and loud laughter.

"Hey. We found the party," said James.

"My tenant," said Olivia, knowing otherwise. "It'll break up soon. 'Night."

She knocked on Dee's door. He might have been standing there waiting for her, he opened it so fast. "What's going on up there?"

"No idea," he said. "It's been like this all night."

"My God. Did you ask them to shut up?"

"Of course not. For all I knew, you'd invited them."

"Dee. Wouldn't I have warned you?"

He shrugged. "Everything's new when a best-seller comes to stay. What's pathetic is that I stayed in town to write. Everyone begged me to come away to the mountains, the picturesque off-season Cape, but I refused."

"I'm sorry, Dee. It won't happen again."

"Huh."

You can't control her, he was saying. This whole business is completely out of control.

Just before Olivia came to the top of the stairs, the noise suddenly quieted. A half dozen women she'd never seen before sat alert on the sofas and floor. Plates with scallops of pizza crust were everywhere, crowded by cans of diet soda, glasses of red wine.

Olivia's arrival was not noticed. Every eye was fixed on a figure intensely lit by a battery of photographic lights.

Ryland? What was Ryland doing here?

"The crotch!" a woman cried. "Do the crotch again!"

Olivia blinked. It wasn't Ryland, just someone wearing his jeans, Sox cap, and a Cheshire sweatshirt.

Tucked chin, smoldering Elvis eyes, tongue slowly circling, pelvis thrust out. One hand slid slowly down the fly of Ryland's jeans to weigh and caress a huge bulge.

The women yelled and stamped their feet.

Felicity crouched crablike, the shutter of her camera going like mad.

Shooting Lori.

10

One by one, the women noticed Olivia.

Lori heard their nervous giggles, sensed she'd lost her audience, and tried to peer past the floodlights. Only now did Olivia notice her sling, hard to see because it was the same blue as Ryland's sweatshirt.

Felicity snatched a final shot before rounding angrily on the intruder. "Oh," she said. "It's you."

"Olivia!" cried Lori. "Everybody, this is Olivia. Your hostess."

Make-nice smiles all around, Felicity abstaining, as Olivia repeated names and Lori hastily explained the gathering. "These are the women from Felicity's last workshop, Olivia. The film's still missing, and Felicity decided it was real crucial for everyone to express their feelings. Not just one-on-one, but collectively, within the nurturance of the original group. And guess what? Everyone voted to reconvene tomorrow morning for another workshop. Isn't that great?"

"Great," said Olivia. "Right now, though, let's wind it up. The noise is bothering my tenant."

Lori's hand flew to her mouth. "Oh, God, Dee. I forgot about him."

Guilt is contagious. The women jumped up, grabbed for plates and ashtrays. "Gotta change," Lori muttered, "be right back."

Only Felicity stayed aloof from the general flurry, packing her equipment with grim efficiency.

Finally they were gone. Olivia washed glasses—they'd used the crystal that didn't go in the dishwasher—and Lori, talking constantly, cleared away the rest.

Felicity had phoned right after Olivia left. Professional anxieties and home-alone blues proving a fertile mix, everything had fallen quickly into place. "The idea was, Come meet a famous novelist, enjoy an evening in a posh Beacon Hill town house. Which did the trick, because look how all six showed up. Last-minute, Friday-night—it's kind of amazing. But of course the really amazing thing was what happened at the photo session. And to think it was totally spontaneous! God! Gives me the shivers."

Spontaneous. Much as Olivia wanted to run to bed and pull the covers over her head, this was a stopper. "Felicity just happened to be lugging her lights and camera along?"

Lori laughed. "I'm not explaining right. She came prepared, of course. The idea was, she'd take some publicity stills. They're always useful, maybe even for the cover of *Follow Me*. Anyway, after a while people started talking about the workshop, discussing their visactualization polarities, and we sort of slipped into mine—what my polarities might be, I mean. It was incredible, Olivia. You know what I ended up with? Soldier/ sexpot. You walked in on Sexpot."

"I guessed."

Lori giggled. "Soldier was kind of inevitable, I guess—my identification with Kate, the central character in *Follow Me*. Writing plays into Soldier too. The basic process of writing. You get an order from this authority down deep in your soul and you have to obey. No arguments, no stopping to ask why. You have to do it, and you have to be brave. You have to accept the reality that you can be wounded with no advance warning. You can get reviews that cut you to shreds. Or someone you thought was a friend goes around saying mean things about your books. But you keep marching on, no matter what. So Soldier was a natural.

"Sexpot, though—that was a real surprise to me. First I came up with Free Spirit. Felicity's like, free to be *what*? It took forever, but finally I stumbled into this amazing new place in my head. I wanted the sexuality of a fifteen-year-old boy. You know, total hormones, stick it in, pow, get it off. No fuss, no consequences. It was such a rush! Incredible. Except . . . I'm really sorry I upset you, Olivia."

"I'm not upset." A lie.

"You didn't mind it was Ryland's clothes? Because I can see how, that wad of socks and all . . ."

"Forget it," said Olivia, wondering when she herself would.

"I thought we'd be done before you came home."

Eerily, horribly, this was pure Ryland. What Mom doesn't know can't hurt her. Olivia gritted her teeth. "That still leaves Dee. He'd counted on a quiet evening to get some writing done."

"I'm really sorry. I'll apologize to him first thing tomorrow. Or should I call right now?"

"Suit yourself. I'm going to hit the hay."

"We weren't that noisy, you know. Except for the photo session. It kind of fired them up. Writer bares soul, blah, blah."

Olivia had to ask. "Any second thoughts on that?"

"Gosh no! I feel great. It's amazing—with those lights and all, Felicity snapping away, my wrist hardly hurt at all. Like it was a healing, you know? And you know something else? For the first time in a long time, I can't wait for tomorrow morning. Power up the old Mac, belt out a fast ten pages on Kate at boot camp. Take off from that momentum to polish up the chapters I did before and fire them off to Pia. Wow. Can I actually do that? Wow. I think I can. I really think so, Olivia!"

She flung her good arm around Olivia, gave her an energetic hug. "I wouldn't be ready without your help, you know. Oh, yes, definitely. This one's yours."

Hug back, Olivia instructed herself, it's silver-lining time.

"Oh," Lori then remembered. "Your son called. Abbott. He said to tell you he'll call tomorrow morning."

Trouble? Unlike his younger brother, Abbott was a letter-writer, not a phoner. "You catch any disaster vibes?"

"Exact opposite. And wow, does he sound grown up. Is he?"

"Most of the time."

"Incredible. Rob had these names for them. Caster and something."

Olivia was astonished. Rob hadn't seemed the kind of neighbor to notice kids, much less give them special names. "Castor and Pollux?"

"That's it. You know them?"

"It's Greek mythology. The heavenly twins. The Gemini."

"Oh. I wonder what would've happened if Rob and I had kids. We tried, you know. Years ago."

"I thought he had a vasectomy."

A complicated smile. "That was just talk. He has immotile sperm. He'd kill me if he knew I told you that. Remember how he said to pack my diaphragm? We didn't have that much of a sex life, but he always made sure I was wearing it. Total denial, you know?"

"You're well away from him, Lori."

Now her smile was natural, guileless. "I know."

The kitchen skylight poured sun. A beautiful day, auspicious for Lori's plunge back into her novel, which might be taking place this precise minute. Early as it was, she was definitely awake; Olivia had heard the shower.

And what, Olivia asked herself, will you do today? Have some more coffee? Why, yes, thanks, that would be lovely. Then what? Wait for Abbott's call before hitting Mikey's? Sounds good. And then? No idea. Does that worry you? Not in the least.

Goodness. To what do we owe this extraordinary contentment?

Goodness, apologies to Mae West, had lots to do with it. The Kasarjians' dining room is good because I'm a good decorator. Also, I had a good time last night.

Because James Warriner is good company?

Yes, but remember: James Warriner is very young.

Yes, but winter's coming. And contentment's warming.

The phone rang. Abbott. Who, before he'd state his business, demanded to know who had answered the phone last night.

"Lori Lutz. Remember she used to live near us? No? Well, she's having big trouble with her husband, so I invited her to stay awhile."

"Where's she sleeping?"

"Why ask? You're the neat and tidy one, your room gets the guests."

Silence from New Hampshire.

"Abbott? Do you really mind? I put your treasures safely away."

"Will she be there for Thanksgiving?"

"No. This is just stopgap. Until she gets her finances settled."

"Oh. Because Thanksgiving's why I called, Mom. Is it okay if I bring a friend home?"

"Sure."

"Really?"

"Of course. Tell your friend he's welcome."

"She. Orawan. Never mind her last name, it's totally unpronounceable. She's from Bangkok. This is her first year, so she's pretty homesick. Plus, all she knows about America is New Hampshire. She's got to get some real-world exposure. Her roommate invited her to New York, this ritzoid Park Avenue apartment, but I said that was crazy."

Olivia heard Lori's step, coming upstairs.

"I agree. Start with Boston, work up to New York. Tell her if she knows how to make pad thai, I'd like lessons."

They said good-bye and hung up. Preoccupied by this weirdly recurrent Bangkok motif, as well as thoughts of her son, who'd never yet brought home a girlfriend or friend-who-was-a-girl, she was slow to notice Lori's red eyes, the druggy way she dropped into her chair. "What's wrong?"

"My book's gone. Rob erased it and left me this." She handed Olivia a piece of paper.

Your army book sucks, Olivia read. *Repent and sin no more.* "I don't understand."

Lori, done in, could hardly speak. "I opened the folder on my hard disk. It was empty. Then I tried the backup copies, and all I found was the note. He erased everything."

Olivia had a Mac too; she knew Lori was talking about an electronic folder and copies, not the kind you can hold in your hands. "Was Rob here? In this house?"

"No. It's revenge for when I changed my mind about coming home."

"You mean the first night you stayed here? But—"

"Oh, God, this is so embarrassing. I lied about my one-handed typing. The truth is, until this morning I never even powered up. I couldn't. Just the thought of it made me so sick and dizzy I had to take a pill, lie down and rest. I guess because so much was riding on this book. Like those couple of hundred pages were all that stood between me and total disaster. But I'm really *really* sorry I lied to you."

"Where's the printout?"

"I never print first drafts. Printing locks you in. I like knowing everything's fluid, just a bunch of electrons or whatever they are."

Her pride in this theory of composition delayed Olivia's full understanding of Rob's treachery. Then it hit: The book was *gone*. What Pia Rosato in New York was waiting for so impatiently no longer existed. Professionally and financially—no manuscript, no advance—Lori was in limbo. "Let me get this straight. Rob erased your book before either of you had said out loud that your marriage was over?"

Lori nodded tearfully.

"I can't deal with it," Olivia said. "The man's inhuman. Forget that he's your husband, for a writer to destroy another writer's work—" She couldn't finish. Then: "Wait. It's not *really* destroyed, is it? I mean, you did it once, you can do it again. You don't have to start from scratch."

"I don't? It sure feels that way. I've been trying to remember sequences and stuff and it's a total blank."

"Could that be the painkillers you're taking? Or the shock of Rob's malice? Maybe in a few days . . ."

"Yeah."

Hearing hopelessness, Olivia shut up.

A long weepy silence, then Lori dashed at her eyes, banged the table with an angry fist. "I hate this *crying*."

"You've been hurt, you can cry all you want."

"No. Felicity's right. Crying's for victims. A woman can choose to go down in tears or she can choose empowerment and action. Last night, visactualizing, that was *me*, Olivia. The *real* me. I'm a person who takes *action*."

She sat tall, her reddened eyes flashing. "Rob chose to hurt me. It's a choice he's made many times before. Like Felicity says, undermining's his game, destruction's his aim. But if I no longer choose to be his victim, everything changes. He can't win unless I choose to lose. It's that simple."

Olivia murmured supportively. Lori's book, her lifeline to

the future, had been snatched away, its retrieval highly problematic. If clutched straws would get her through this dark day, let her clutch. "I'm going to the Spa for the paper," she said. "Want to keep me company?"

"I can't. I mean, God. Look at me."

"It's just your eyes. Wear sunglasses."

"No. You go ahead. I'll be fine."

"Sure? Okay. Back in a jiffy."

Returning, Olivia found a note: *Gone to Felicity's. See you Sunday PM.* A jiffy, obviously, had been plenty of time for Lori to choose action over tearful despair.

11

From that weekend emerged a changed Lori, pumped, constantly on the move. No pretext of writing, no mention of her stolen book. Instead of joining Olivia for meals, she'd be off having lunch with Boy or the Lyman House fund-raising committee, then meet Felicity or some of the visactualizers for dinner. Lingering affairs, these; she'd roll in around midnight.

"It's like I've hatched from a cocoon," she marveled to Olivia in transit. "I mean, wherever I go, there's all this *life*. Two of Felicity's women have been through basically the same horror show as me and Rob. I'm getting these really amazing insights on the, you know, victim/empowerment nexus."

Her absences and late hours suited Olivia just fine, especially after Mary Jane Hughes called to report that Lori had contacted exactly one lawyer on the list, and then neither shown for the appointment she'd made nor called to cancel.

"I apologize for her rudeness," Olivia said. "And for getting you into this."

"You don't sound surprised," Mary Jane said.

"She lies a lot. Was it a woman she stood up?"

"No. Why?"

"She told me she'd talked to two women. Fans of her books,

she said. Doesn't matter. Lawyer or no, she's out of here by Thanksgiving."

Saying this to Mary Jane, Olivia knew it was firm, set in stone. The persuader had been Lori's remarkable recovery from the loss of her book. Whatever else, the woman was resilient. Orawan, Abbott's friend, was an unassailable pretext: Gee, Lori, we need the room, and by the way, don't come back after the holiday. For all Olivia knew, Lori might be secretly relieved. Can't be much fun, getting caught in a major lie. But even if she minded her ouster, or found it inconvenient, she'd bounce. Find someone new—Boy, Felicity, a visactualizer—to take her in.

Meantime, there was James Warriner. Olivia had thought he'd call in a couple of weeks. Or leave the next move to her. Instead, he called first thing Monday morning, encouraging her to leap boldly into chartless space and pick dinner over a safety-first lunch.

A Friday-night date with a Republican. What next?

The day before this intriguing event, Olivia woke to hear the stairs creak under Dee's departing feet. Tuesdays and Thursdays he taught an eight-o'clock class in Freshman Composition. "Heavy lifting," he'd described it. "A brutal subject at an evil hour."

She was brushing her teeth when the doorbell started, long, insistent rings, the kind you know will never quit. Had Dee forgotten something, managed to lock himself out? Yeah, yeah, yeah, she grumbled, running to the intercom.

"Police, Mrs. Chapman. Detective McGuire, remember me? I need to talk to you."

She remembered McGuire very well; last summer he'd questioned her after person or persons unknown put some bullets in a Chapman Interiors client. "I just woke up. Can't it wait?"

"It really can't, Mrs. Chapman. I'll just hang on your stoop, okay? Out of the rain, more or less."

"Five minutes," she said.

McGuire had gained weight. The cap, too, made a change from summer. A Greek fisherman's cap, of all peculiar choices, rain beading its meager brim.

Once the door was shut behind him, the foyer, big enough for a boot bench and two normal people, turned claustrophobic.

Should they move to her office? No. The sixties were gone but not entirely forgotten. Fuzz and personal space don't mix.

The moment for a handshake had passed, mostly because McGuire had been getting out his notebook, carefully turning its damp pages. Besides, whatever this was, it wasn't social. Olivia attempted friendly candor. "I can't quite say Nice to see you again."

"I know the problem. I'm here because a woman over on Chestnut Street—Mrs. Keaton, Willa Keaton—told me you've got Lori Lutz staying with you. That so?"

"Yes. She's upstairs right now." Was she? Olivia had no idea.

"You saw her this morning?"

"No. She's still asleep. Unless you woke her ringing the bell like that."

"What'd she have, a late night?"

"I guess. She had dinner out, with friends. I was asleep when she came home—didn't hear her. What's this about?"

"Her husband. Mrs. Keaton was out early with her dog. No leash, so the dog went for those big bushes in Mr. Mallory's front yard. Barked up a storm when he found him."

Olivia stared. "Found Rob? What do you mean?"

"He's dead. Wounds to the chest and neck. Knife left at the scene, for all the help that gives us."

Olivia dropped onto the bench. "I can't believe this."

McGuire's nod was sympathetic. "Kind of thing you don't usually see in neighborhoods like this, God be thanked."

"Street crime, you mean? Robbery?"

"What do you think, Mrs. Chapman?"

"Rob Mallory's the feisty type. Was. I bet he'd fight back if someone jumped him. He'd yell. Did anyone hear a fight?"

"The officers are asking. You knew him pretty well?"

"We'd say hello on the street, maybe chat briefly. My feelings about him have changed since Lori came here, of course. She had to leave home because she was afraid for her life."

"I'm ready to talk to Mrs. Lutz now, Mrs. Chapman."

Olivia remembered this, too, the way McGuire sidestepped a citizen's questions and comments. Irritated, she stood, her decision made. "Lori's been through a lot lately. I won't wake her for you unless I can break the news myself—try to cushion the shock."

McGuire shrugged. "Fine with me."

Olivia indicated the bench. "Have a seat. And call her Ms. Lutz, okay? Not *Mrs.*"

Old-school McGuire rolled his eyes.

The shuttered bedroom smelled strongly of the Dial soap Lori had taken to using. She lay sprawled on her back, mouth agape, snoring slightly. Dead to the world, Olivia thought before she caught herself.

God help me, she thought, the enormity of murder filling her head like cold fog. How to do this?

"Lori? Yo, Lori. Wake up."

No response. She switched on the bedside lamp, saw, on the table, her splint, and, spread out neatly, the blue sling.

The splint looked unusually clean. Without thinking, Olivia touched it, felt dampness. She bent close, got a noseful of Dial. From the sling, too. Unfastidious Lori doing hand laundry in the middle of the night? With one hand?

Next to the splint were two prescription containers with

their lids off. Percocet, one label said, for pain. The other, Restoril, was for sleeping. She knew nothing about Restoril, but Percocet was dealt on the street. People used it to change the look and feel of standard reality.

Heart wild in her chest, Olivia saw herself tearing down to McGuire, pouring it all out in a breathless spill: Lori's hopeless financial position; one, if not two, suspect drugs; her nighttime prowlings; Felicity's nutty theories urging action—

She forced her attention back to concrete reality, to peaceful, defenseless Lori and explanations less sensational. The splint and sling had become too grubby, even for her. When was she supposed to wash them if not at night?

She shook Lori's shoulder, tentatively at first, then with urgency and conviction.

Finally Lori's eyes flew open. "Wha— What's going on?"

"I'm sorry I had to startle you," Olivia said. "You've got to get up. Something's happened."

"I couldn't sleep," Lori moaned, rolling onto her side. "Had to take an extra pill."

"There's a police detective downstairs. He wants to talk to you about Rob."

"Why? He beat someone else up?"

"Willa Keaton found him under your front bushes. He's dead, Lori. He was stabbed."

Lori sat up, blankets clutched protectively to her chest. "*No.*"

Olivia was pure wonderment. "Well, would you look at that."

It was a moment before Lori realized she'd grabbed for the blankets with both hands. "Oops," she said. Peering up through her lashes, she tried for naughty. Little kid caught in the cookie jar, too cute to be punished.

Faced with murder, she can summon cute? What was going on here? Olivia let fly. "Faking all along, were you?"

"Of course not! Go ask at Mass. General!"

"I wouldn't waste my time," said Olivia, much tutored by her sons' athletic injuries. "Sprains don't show on X rays. Pain's whatever you claim. You can easily fake the strength test, and if you blow the rest—reflexes, hot, cold, whatever, they write it up as confused neurological response. Doesn't matter. They splint you and dose you same as for real."

"I wish you'd been there, Olivia. I wish you'd heard my agony in that emergency room."

"Speaking of agony, you're taking Rob's murder right in stride."

"That's not fair! First you're mad at me for faking, and then you want me to fake."

A valid point. Olivia conceded it.

"I can't even *tell* how I feel," Lori went on. "I was crazy in love with him for years and years. He worked me over, turned every last smidge of love into fear and hate. Am I glad he can't hurt me anymore? Yes. I might fall apart later, but right now that's where I am—glad. I'm going to have to watch myself with the cops."

Her eyes shone with what might be tears of relief, even joy. "I'm free," she cried, "I've lucked out!"

Olivia turned practical. "You've got to get dressed. The longer McGuire waits, the worse it looks for you."

"What're you talking about?"

Olivia kept it simple. "You have plenty of reasons for wanting him dead. You were out last night. Anyone can buy a knife—I've seen real serious ones at Eddie Bauer, for God's sake. You're strong, about Rob's size. The surprise element's important too. Anyone jumping him would have an edge, but you've got extra. He sees you, thinks doormat, down goes his guard. You come on like a pit bull, and before he can adjust, he's dead."

"I didn't kill him. Honest. You've got to believe me, Olivia."

"McGuire's the one who has to believe you."

Lori went sly. "What about my wrist? If the cops think it's

still sprained they'll know I couldn't stab anyone. A one-armed woman can't take on a man—not without him doing some serious damage back. And look at me. No bruises, scratches. Nothing but"—her little smile, her entire self, became a desperate plea—"a bad sprain."

Olivia weighed it.

"Don't hate me, Olivia. Please."

"I hate lying. And being conned."

"I can relate. No, really. In your shoes, I'd feel no different. But can you relate to how it was for me? The bad wrist is key. It's basically why you took me in. Because how well did we know each other back then? Weren't you taking a risk with me? And didn't my injury kind of make up for the risk?"

"To a degree."

"So when it started getting better, I got scared you'd kick me out. Not per se, but sort of like, you know, Hey Lori, maybe you'd be more comfortable with a place of your own. And I wasn't ready for that. Nowhere near. Even if I had the money, which I don't."

"You do now."

It was still a new idea. Lori's grin dazzled. "Yeah. I do."

Money and a home she could go to. Now. Weeks before Olivia had planned to kick her out.

Freedom, in other words, with no hard feelings at the end. All Olivia had to do was support the lie about the splint, burden her own conscience to offer Lori one last helping hand.

Or she could tell the straight-arrow truth, spare her conscience the burden of lying, and watch what developed from the seed of suspicion she'd inevitably plant in McGrath's mind. How long would it take him to discover more of Lori's lies? And how would those discoveries undermine Lori's claim of innocence?

An impossible debate, leading only to brain fog and paralysis. Olivia had to decide, right now.

Between two evils, Mae West once advised, always pick the one you haven't tried yet.

"Put on the splint," she told Lori. "I won't say a word."

"You've been awhile, Mrs. Chapman. She took it bad?"

"The shock, yes. She'll be down soon. I'm right next door if you want me."

She left the inner foyer door open, her office door, too. The helpful eavesdropper.

As the minutes dragged, Olivia considered Lori's sunrise grin, that moment of fresh awareness that her troubles were over. Was this proof of her innocence? Or only a lie told in body language? Put differently, if Lori hadn't killed Rob, who had? A hireling she'd found? That tough-sounding guy, maybe, who'd asked for Mrs. Lori? Or did Felicity know people, have a rent-a-thug section in her Rolodex? Also, what about Lori's newfound soul sisters, the visactualizers of the victim/empowerment nexus? *A woman can choose to go down in tears or she can choose empowerment and action.* Violent action, why not? One choice among others, no big deal.

Was Boy a candidate? Boy loves Lori, Lori yawns, says prove it, Boy slays dragon?

Lori, finally, was coming downstairs.

12

Lori was wearing her olive-green outfit. Olivia gave her a reassuring wave, but wondered at the gamble. Dressed elegantly and expensively, Lori might seem free of financial motives to kill, but the instant the police checked Rob's accounts, they'd know better.

McGuire started by saying he was sorry to bring news like this. Too quickly, cutting him off, Lori said it was a terrible shock, terrible. "And of course I'm upset and sorry that Rob's dead," she plunged breathlessly on. "Whatever he did to me, he didn't deserve this. You heard, right? Why I had to move out?"

McGuire asked for details, and Lori produced a plenitude, overdoing, in Olivia's estimation, Exhibit A, her sprain, and the irksome ways it hampered her every waking act.

Some fencing followed, Lori pushing for who-what-why-when, McGuire sticking to her movements of the night before. Told she routinely roamed the night streets alone, he expressed surprise. "If I don't walk, I can't sleep," Lori said. "Anyway, in comparison to facing blank sheets of paper, what's to worry?"

McGuire laughed. "I'll pass that on to my wife. She's got all your books."

After some backing and filling on why he himself never found time to read and how much he regretted this sorry state of affairs, McGuire returned to last night. Lori named the women she'd drunk beer and eaten chili with in the Sevens, down on Charles Street. "I left around eleven-fifteen, maybe a little later."

"Mrs. Chapman didn't hear you come in."

"I guess. I took the long way, which is basically the perimeter of the Public Garden and Common."

"You see any friends? Speak to anyone?"

"God, no. I never do, really."

"You're a well-known person, been on TV and all. People must recognize you, huh?"

"Well, see, that's the problem. There was a time in my life when I'd go to places like Cheers, you know, tourist places. I'd meet fans from all over the country, and it was good publicity. I stopped because—well, people mix things up. They think me and my characters are one and the same, you know? They're like, Wow, I feel so close to you, it's like you're my best friend. But of course I'm not, nowhere near. I'm basically, Whoa, this is too close, get me out of here. It shows. Leaves a bad taste. The Sevens is great. No tourists, and the locals could care. Out walking, I basically schlump along, grubby old clothes, no eye contact. I guess someone could have recognized me last night. I mean, it's possible. But unless they spoke to me, I'd be the last to notice."

"You get yourself caught in this rain, Ms. Lutz?"

"It was just spitting. Sure is coming down now. Is that bad for footprints and stuff?"

McGuire grunted. "Anything else you can tell me? Names of people who might've had problems with your husband?"

Lori's sigh was plaintive. "Lots of people had problems with Rob. He, uh, spoke his mind. But did anyone hate him? I don't know."

"I have to ask, Ms. Lutz. Was there a girlfriend?"

Olivia gulped. Should she speak up? Sock Lori with Kim on top of everything else?

"A girlfriend." Lori seemed to be trying the concept on for size. "No. At least I don't know of one. Like I said, that wasn't why I left."

"You've started divorce proceedings?"

"Yes, but Rob ignores the letters."

Olivia, hardly breathing, had to admire this.

Lori impatiently ticked her tongue. "I keep using the wrong tense. The thing is, I was Rob's meal ticket. One hundred percent. He wasn't in any hurry to change things."

"I assume it was your money that bought the house? That's hard, Ms. Lutz. You're camping out, he has the run of a nice big place he didn't even pay for."

"I'm not complaining. I like it here. Olivia's been great and the food's fantastic. Even with two working arms I can't cook worth squat. Course, home is home. When can I move back?"

"When we're done. It's a big place. We'll want to be thorough."

"For sure. Some creep's out there killing people . . . God! Makes my skin crawl. Wait. What about Bingo? Rob's cat."

"The officers fed him. He was acting kind of wild, they said."

"That's Bingo."

Sounding ready to leave, McGuire told Lori to call if she thought of anything else or heard anything around the neighborhood. She'd hear from them soon about the rest. "We've got his license photo, yeah, wallet in his pocket, a fifty and two twenties, doesn't look like robbery, but you never know. So your ID's just routine confirmation."

"What?" Lori squeaked. "I have to go to the *morgue*?"

"Only takes a second."

Lori's sobs, harsh, desolate, brought Olivia on the run, her suspicions overcome by a flood of pity.

* * *

Lori had washed her face, changed into sweats, and come upstairs. She accepted Olivia's prescription of cinnamon toast and strong coffee. Then the phone rang.

"The media," she knew to a certainty. "Typical."

"Want me to put them off?" Olivia asked.

"It's okay. They have to do their job. I might as well get it over with."

The caller did most of the talking. From the way Lori listened, it wasn't media, and it wasn't good news. "I'll deny it," she at length said. "Your word against mine."

The caller's response to this bravado was apparently devastating. "It'll take time, but all right," Lori finally said, a world of exhausted defeat in every syllable.

More from the caller. "I *said* all right. You expect me to argue?"

Not waiting for a sign-off, she banged down the receiver. Olivia felt the impact physically.

At that moment, Dee came charging in. "There're cops all over Mount Vernon."

Lori collapsed on the sofa, a wailing ball of misery.

She couldn't tell, she couldn't. She'd been instructed not to breathe a word. "Especially not to you, Olivia."

"Me personally?" Olivia's heart jumped. "My name was used?"

"Don't be mad at me. It's not my fault."

Olivia could smack her. "Forget fault, okay? You're in my house, that puts me in your life. Someone threatens you, I'm threatened, too. So talk. For my sake, if not your own. Nothing has to go outside this room."

"It's not *you*," Lori hastened to say. "I just don't know Dee well enough to, you know . . . No offense, Dee."

"On my way," said Dee, getting up.

"Please, Dee," Olivia said. "Please stay. It's not negotiable, Lori. I can't do a thing for you unless Dee's here to help me."

"But he doesn't, you know, know about me. Does he? I mean, you haven't told him things, have you?"

"'Course not." Olivia let her tone of voice say the rest: You're the liar here, not me. "Dee's quick. He'll fill in fast."

Frowning, Lori rummaged through her options, took a deep breath, began. For a professional storyteller, her first draft was a disorganized mess. Olivia hoped this was because she was trying, for a change, to tell the truth.

Her caller had been Willa Keaton. Last night the Keatons had driven to a suburban party. Gordon having hit the after-dinner brandy too hard, it had fallen to Willa to drive home, deposit Gordon on Chestnut Street, and take the car to the Brimmer Street garage. En route to the garage, on Mount Vernon, she had found a hen's-tooth parking space and grabbed it, preferring to walk a half block home rather than bothering to call a cab from the garage. She was unhooking her seat belt when she saw someone slip out the Lutz/Mallory front door and hurry to the sidewalk. She thought it was Lori, but, titillated, followed her uphill to make sure, reaching Joy in time to see Lori stick her key in Olivia's door. She'd then checked her watch: ten minutes after midnight.

"And now," the outraged innocent concluded, "she's blackmailing me."

Olivia could only stare. "This really happened? You were there?"

"Yeah. I know what you're thinking—"

"*Thinking?* Around you? What's the point?"

From Lori, fresh, raucous despair.

Olivia speechless, Dee took charge, got the tortuous narrative moving again. By degrees Lori confessed that she'd lied to McGuire about her long walk last night. She'd gone straight from the Sevens to her house on Mount Vernon. Further, not many of her nightly rambles had been as extensive as she'd led Olivia to believe. "Basically what I've been doing is scoping out our house. Listen to me, 'our' house. My house. The house I bought and paid for. Okay, anyway, if the lights were on, I'd actually take a walk. But if the house was dark, I'd hunker down in the bushes and wait for Rob to come home. Most of the time he'd be with this woman he's got. The front light's busted, so I never got a good look at her face. She's about his height, just like me, with dark curly hair. That's all I can swear to. He keeps the shades down. A couple of times I heard what could've been fighting, but I didn't catch any words. Okay. Last night, windows dark, I assume no one's home. I duck into my usual hiding place and there's this *thing* right where I put my hand. It was horrible. Course, I didn't know at first it was Rob—it's black as pitch under those bushes. Anyway, it was like I'd touched a live wire. I yanked my hand away, lost my balance and sort of plopped down next to him."

Olivia's mind was going a mile a minute. The woman Lori had described must be Kim. Beyond that, how much of her tale could be trusted? "So that's why you washed your splint," she said.

Lori nodded. "And the rest of my clothes. A female plus, right? You get expert with blood. Not that I found that much to wash. There was some mud, of course. Anyway, better safe than sorry. I washed everything."

"How do you know you didn't leave bloodstains in the house?" Olivia asked. "Track it in on your shoes?"

"So what if I did? It's Rob's blood, not mine." A complicated smirk. "And don't worry about what I tracked in here. I took my sneakers off the minute I got inside. I washed them with the rest of my stuff, but before I went to bed I thought, hey, why not just toss them? Today's trash day, right? Those sneakers were on their way to the dump before McGuire ever got here."

Dee wanted to get back to Rob. "Was Rob cold and stiff? When you found him?"

Lori grimaced. "I don't think so. But it's not like I really checked. I just lay there trying to calm down. It was so weird, me puffing like a racehorse, Rob so still. Part of me's like,

You'll never hurt me again, but then I'd have to jam my fist in my mouth to keep from screaming. See?"

She showed them the marks around her knuckles. "And that's through gloves. Remember when McGuire said I had to go to the morgue, Olivia? How I totally lost it? That's what I flashed on—Rob lying there so silent and, you know, helpless."

Olivia broke the silence. "Then you went inside?"

"He never even changed the lock." Astonishment thinned Lori's voice. "Isn't that incredible? I could've gone in any old time I wanted. I could've caught him and Curly in bed. Erased his computer the way he erased mine. Swiped his financial records instead of paying my lawyer to pull teeth one by one."

My lawyer? Olivia nonplussed, it fell to Dee to ask the obvious question. "The man's dead. Why risk implicating yourself?"

"What, you think I *planned* this? I was in shock! Automatic pilot! Maybe I was looking for some note that would explain everything, who knows. Anyway, I sort of woke up in his study. Okay. His Mac's running, and on the screen is all this kinky sex. Two characters, 'Rob' and 'K.' I'll spare you the grisly details, but all I could think was, people, the cops and all, will think this is *us*. Like his other abuse was only the tip of the iceberg. Like, What's she expect, playing these sicko sex games. Asking for it, right?"

Olivia and Dee exchanged a glance. Yup. People, the cops and all, surely will do just that.

Lori nodded, grim but gratified. "So I dumped the whole thing on a floppy and brought it back here. Sat up half the night reading."

"Fingerprints," said Dee. "On his keyboard."

"No. I'd run down to the kitchen for my rubber gloves. Look, could I just get to the end of this? He was writing in the form of a diary. Really creepy. I mean, I'm the first to admit that certain aspects of this stuff can be a turn-on. You know, Take me, do whatever you want with me, all that. . . . Like

Felicity says, the female archetype craves surrender. She fantasizes oceanic forces beyond her personal capacity to resist. But this version of Rob's . . . He's playing for keeps, you know? The only way this story's going to end is with K dead. So I started to think, who's K?"

"Kurt," declared Dee with donnish satisfaction, referring to the monstrous father in Rob's novel.

Lori shook her head. "Never. The Rob character's got the whip."

"Different sides, same coin," Dee proposed.

It's time, Olivia knew. "I ran into Rob and a woman friend on the street. Dark curly hair, about his height. He made a point of introducing us. Her name's Kim Amundsen."

"What? Why didn't you tell me?"

"I wouldn't have told you now if Kim didn't start with a K."

"That's the *pits*, Olivia. You had no right!"

Olivia said nothing.

"This is totally insane," Lori steamed on. "What else are you hiding from me? Huh?"

Dee whooped. "Sorry. Sheer effrontery always turns me giddy."

"What's he talking about?" Lori crossly demanded.

"You're the one who hides things," Olivia said, stifling a powerful impulse to list every last lie and evasion.

"At least until your blackmailer called," Dee added. "What's Willa's deal?" Olivia asked. "Not money, surely."

"No. She won't tell the police she saw me if Boy puts Lyman House in another part of town."

Olivia was very dry. "And you agreed."

"Did I have a choice? She said she'd pass the lie-detector test and I'd fail."

"That's crazy," Olivia said. "Those tests are notoriously inconclusive. You should have denied everything."

Lori shot her a frightening look. "Well, I didn't, okay? It's been kind of a rough morning for me, and I couldn't think that fast."

Down deep, Olivia saw to her chagrin, she doesn't like me much better than I like her.

"Hold it a sec," said Dee. "How can you possibly have that much influence over Boy?"

Lori shrugged. "It's no secret he depends on me emotionally. He tells the world I'm his inspiration and mentor. Basically it's my book—you know, *3 Hots & a Cot*. He goes on and on about how he was drifting aimlessly around the world and then—bam!—he picks it up in this Bangkok guest house and his life's changed. So, yeah, I probably could get him to go for a different venue. The one sure thing is, that woman is desperate to stop the shelter. 'Don't dare underestimate me,' she kept saying, 'I'll do whatever it takes.' "

Remembering Willa at the Kasarjians', Olivia had no trouble believing in her determination. The rest was loony tunes. For one thing, blackmail only works if secret. Of course, Willa was an imperious amateur, not likely to have thought this through, to have realized that the impact of her call might bring other players into the game. Also, there was a huge gaping hole on Lori's side of the bargain. "Okay, Lori. Say you do manage to persuade Boy. What guarantee do you have that Willa will keep her mouth shut forever?"

Lori, sullen and silent, obviously hadn't considered this.

"You'd better call McGuire," Olivia went on. "Come clean."

Lori gave a scornful laugh. "Obviously you've never had trouble with the law. I have. Kid stuff, back in Carbondale—boosting lipsticks in the Rite-Aid, breaking into houses to snoop around, eat their ice cream, steal their booze. One basic reason I left home so young. The cops wouldn't get off my case."

"You have a record?" Dee was dead serious.

"Most of it's sealed. Juvenile. Doesn't matter. I could've grown up in a convent, they'll be all over me on this. Like that Willa kept saying, the spouse is suspect number one, always and always. Plus, Rob's dead, who has more to gain?"

Dee frowned. "How can a woman with a sprained wrist—"

Olivia interrupted. "Suppose they find fibers or something under the bushes. That poncho of yours is pretty distinctive."

"I think she's all right there," said Dee. "They lived in the same house, bound to be mingling. Also, from what I read in the paper, Boston's forensic lab is a mess. Takes forever to get things analyzed, no end of evidence gets lost in the process."

"Look, I didn't kill him. You both know that, so—"

The phone rang. "I can't talk," Lori said. "To anyone."

Olivia answered. It was a reporter from Channel 6, a woman unwilling to take no for an answer.

"She's had a shock, and she's not ready to talk," Olivia said for the third time. "That's all I can tell you."

The reporter tried a new tack. "She's your friend? You want to help her? Then tell her to hold a press conference. That's best with this kind of thing."

"What kind of thing, specifically?"

"She's famous. People love her books. If they don't already know why she left home, they will soon, and they'll be anxious to hear her side. Otherwise, how can they *take* her side?"

Olivia said she'd pass this along, noted the reporter's name and number, and hung up.

With breathtaking speed, and a single call to Felicity, it was settled. Lori would indeed hold a press conference, at Felicity's loft, right after her visit to the morgue. "She says I should do it today," Lori informed Olivia and Dee. "Get it over with, and they'll go easy on the new widow. One-thirty, Felicity said. Gives them time to eat lunch, but plenty of leeway to make the six o'clock news. Felicity'll call the major outlets, but she wants an announcement on your machine, Olivia. I'll go type one up.

Wait. A man's voice would be good. Could you tape it for me, Dee? Great. Be right back."

"Why do we stand aghast?" Dee murmured to Olivia. "Folks in remote Tehran and Tiananmen Square understood how to service the media; why should Lori and Felicity be caught lacking?"

Emotional whiplash, Olivia decided. That's what she was suffering from. The horror of McGuire's news, *whip;* the secondary shock of Lori's faked sprain, *whip;* her own suffusion of pity, *whip;* Willa's blackmail threat and all it had exposed.

In the morass, one steady rock. "I meant it when I said I needed your help, Dee. Did you hear her come home last night?"

"Not a peep. Think she killed him?"

"Let's talk. Soon as she goes to Felicity's."

"Fine," said Dee.

"What's fine?" asked Lori, coming into the room.

"Burgers for lunch," said Olivia.

"Nothing for me," said Lori. "Butterflies in my stomach." She handed Dee his lines. "This okay?"

He scanned the page, penciled some changes, handed it back.

"Wow!" exclaimed Lori. "That's so much better! Thanks a million."

Dee going to the machine to dictate, Olivia drew Lori into the kitchen and went for the morning's simplest loose end. "Why didn't you tell me you had a lawyer?"

Some trademark evasion, then: "I only hired him last week. He's not on that list or anything."

"I know. Mary Jane checked around."

"Oh, boy. You're mad again. I couldn't . . . Look, I know Rob. He'd make mincemeat out of . . . This man I picked, Pappas, he's kind of a kneecapper, you know? I was afraid to tell you because you'd be like, What's with this slimebag? Like I'm a slimebag, too, you know?"

"Jesus, Lori." Olivia was protesting the truth buried in this charge as much as anything else. But Lori, distracted by Dee's playback check, either didn't hear or didn't care. "You'd better call him," she went on.

"Call Pappas? Why?"

"He's out of a job."

"Oh. Right. God, what's wrong with me? I keep forgetting the silver lining."

13

Murder having nipped his divorce fee in the bud, Lori's kneecapper argued strenuously for a role at the press conference. "It's real nice of you to offer," she finally said, "but no. Having you there, any lawyer, I'm basically waving a red flag. Admitting I need a, you know, mouthpiece, because I've got something to hide. Which of course I don't."

Rid of Pappas at last, Lori insisted on detailing his every effort to "muscle in." Olivia murmured responses, Dee didn't bother. The rain punished the skylights. The silence of the phone seemed malevolent, as if new horrors in the outside world were overwhelming any possibility of communication.

Olivia was desperate to talk to Dee, no holds barred, but Lori seemed in no hurry to leave them alone.

"So," she now said, "you guys going to tell on me or what?"

Cute-kid wheedling. Dee refused to be enchanted. "I need time to think. Blackmail's not something I grapple with on a daily basis."

"There's too much at stake for snap decisions," Olivia added. "Boy's dream—"

"*Boy's* dream?" Lori's eyes narrowed. "Without me, it wouldn't exist. Anyway, I'm only asking him to relocate, not ditch it. Who's going to care? Not the target group, that's for sure. One thing about the homeless, they're mobile."

"Boy will care," said Olivia. "That house symbolizes family wrongdoing and his own atonement. The rest of the board will care, and so will the people who've signed on to raise money. Lyman House involves their whole vision of what Beacon Hill ought to strive toward. Michelle Greene will certainly care. She calls Lyman House her site-specific freebie."

Lori scowled. "What's that supposed to mean?"

"She was hooked by one particular architectural entity. Normally she doesn't volunteer professional services—it's been a firm principle of hers. So, right, the homeless are mobile, but don't count on anyone else."

"Including you?" asked Lori.

"I go with Michelle."

Angrily: "Even though I put you two together."

"Yes."

"Too bad you don't care about me as much as these other people."

"I do care about you. That's why this is such a tough call."

Lori drew a deep breath, let it out slowly. "Why are we fighting? For all we know, the cops are closing in on the killer right this minute."

Bounce. The woman was remarkable. "Not to kick you out," Olivia was emboldened to say, "but Dee and I need to talk."

Lori got to her feet fast. "No problem. I was thinking, this rain and all, I should hustle over to Felicity's. Let her fool with my hair, slap on some war paint. Look my best, right?"

"First run down and get the diary," Dee said.

"What? You can't read that thing."

"Why not?"

"I said! You'll mix me up in it. You'll be like, Wow, kinky on this scale can't come out of the blue, Rob must've *practiced*."

Dee's gaze was level, passionless. "Do stop assuming my responses. It's unpleasant, and you lack qualification."

Lori's mouth fell open in astonishment. Olivia told herself she wasn't Mom here, she didn't have to make peace.

"Time's a-wasting," Dee said. "Let's have it. Bring the disk, too."

Lori bit back further argument and flounced off as bidden. Returning, she tossed the printout and disk carelessly onto the sofa.

"Should go quickly," Dee predicted, leafing through. "Short sentences, lots of dialogue."

"You expect me to sit here and watch?" Lori made it an accusation.

"Not unless you want," said Dee.

"Go," said Olivia. "Good luck at the press conference."

"You get nightmares from that filth," Lori threw over her shoulder, "don't blame me. Don't say I didn't warn you."

"What was all that about you and Michelle Greene?" Dee asked, killing time until Lori was safely gone.

Olivia explained her decision to get involved with Lyman House. "And no ragging from you," she warned. "This is a smart professional move, not dewy-eyed charity."

"You're like Henry of Navarre," said Dee. "No? He was a Protestant. 'Turn RC,' they said, 'and you can be King of France.' 'Show me where to sign,' he said, 'Paris is well worth a Mass.' A thoroughly professional response. He proved a decent king."

They heard the street door slam.

Dee pounced. "She kill him?"

"She could have. The sprain's long cured, I discovered this morning. Yeah, I know. She was afraid she'd lose my sympathy."

"Coony, my mother would call her. Sly and knowing."

"To a point. She really blew it with Willa. Should've gone all huffy and law-abiding, turned the tables on her. But: Did she kill him? God knows she had motive. As Felicity expressed it, undermining was his game, destruction his aim. He abused her physically—"

"She says."

"He was vicious to her the day we picked up her stuff. And I saw him torment her on the deck, remember? His choke-chain routine? Anyway, it's beyond dispute that he defrauded her on a massive scale. This'll be new to you: He paid cash, hers, for the house. And guess what? Only one name's on the deed."

"I find it *so* hard to have compassion for the truly stupid."

"She says she did it for love," Olivia told him.

"She says."

Time out while the phone rang and did its thing. A reporter's voice promised to be at the press conference.

"He erased the book she was working on," Olivia said.

This got Dee's attention, but when Olivia had finished explaining, he repeated his mantra. "She says."

"Oh, please," said Olivia. "She erased her own book?"

Dee's shrug was world-weary. He'd seen worse.

Olivia reconsidered Lori's astonishing recovery that morning, the way she'd bounced off to Felicity, light and quick as a Ping-Pong ball. It wasn't hard to construct a new scenario. Lori powers up for the first time in weeks, starts reading with new, visactualized eyes. Finds nothing more than trite confusion, soulless blabber. Scrolls ahead, same result. And again. Still nothing worth revising, building on. Until, inescapably, it's decision time. Does she opt for brave, steady Soldier and push on against crushing odds? Or does Sexpot, impulsive brat, heedless of consequences, punch DELETE?

She hits DELETE. Yeah! But the high fades fast and aftermath is inevitable. Aghast at what she's done to herself, she breaks down, dumps her woefully burned bridges on credulous Olivia.

And how had she managed to bounce back so fast? Because

within the time-tested gratification of exposing another layer of Rob's malice, Lori had found deep satisfaction in duping Olivia, who thinks she's so smart.

"Penny for your thoughts," said Dee.

As she'd promised Lori, he filled in fast. When she'd finished, though, neither knew positively who had erased the book.

"Her weakest claim," said Dee, "is that he did it that first night."

"Don't forget, I made her call back," said Olivia. "A major thwart. Rob was used to having complete control over her. Getting his own way every time."

"She says. For all we know, the book never existed in the first place."

"My God. You're right."

"Does it matter, though? Can't we simply say these two deserved each other? Certainly you deserve to be shut of the survivor. Immediately, if not before. Can't we leave it at that and get on with our lives?"

Olivia was startled. "Not care who killed him, you mean?"

"Roughly, yes. Course, I'd have to start caring if it turns out random. Random means I might be next."

"If *she'd* been stabbed," Olivia scrupled, "I'd care."

"Personally? You meant it when you told her you cared about her?"

"Sure. Don't you ever have mixed feelings about people? Also, if she'd died, Rob would inherit all her money. That would really stick in my craw. But do I care if Lori killed Rob? Not much. I wouldn't want that spread around, but there it is."

"There it is."

"Also, it's *over*. She hasn't developed some kind of blood lust. She's not going to rampage, stab me in my bed."

"No. Though you might start locking your bedroom door."

"Mm." No point telling Dee she already did. Ever since Lori had introduced Felicity into the household.

Somewhat taken aback by their indifference to the weighty claims of abstract truth and justice, they waited out another interruption from the phone.

"On the other hand," Dee then said.

"Damn. I knew it was too good to last."

"Try this. Would she have gone into the house if she'd killed him?"

"She spazzed out. Or, as you've been so careful to note until this perverse switcheroo, *she says* she spazzed out. Either way, your question's impossible."

"I'm sticking with coony. She wouldn't have gone in. She'd have listened hard for footsteps, cars, picked her moment, melted into the night. I also found myself trusting her description of finding him. The details rang true."

"She's a writer," said Olivia. "Lies for a living."

Dee laughed to have his own logic used against him.

"He's dead, he was a rat, we're out of it," Olivia went on. "That's reality. The rest is only your hunch. And we don't have to do or say a thing about any of this. I know for a fact that citizens are under no legal obligation to volunteer information to the police."

"Really?"

"Yup. At least in Massachusetts."

"Evil flourishes when good men sit back and do nothing."

Olivia smiled. "I'm not a man."

"Tell you what," Dee proposed. "Let's read the filthy screed, then decide."

"Lunch first. In case it spoils my appetite."

The phone rang while Olivia fried their burgers. Another reporter, and then another still. By the end of lunch, they'd quit counting.

Dee's grin was wicked. "How *do* two old friends read porn on a rainy afternoon? Over each other's shoulders?"

"Definitely not." Olivia plunked herself at the other end of the sofa. "You're the speed-reader, you start. Put the pages facedown when you're done, and I'll fish from the bottom."

"Interrupt if something catches you. For any reason."

The first entry was dated the same Saturday as Josie Spangler's wedding in New York. When Olivia pointed this out, Dee flipped to the end. The final entry bore yesterday's date.

"Whatever that tells us," said Dee.

"Since Lori found it on the screen last night, we're in real time. So probably the first entry is real-time too. In which case, he started writing this just before Lori came home from her book tour."

"Unless Lori was lying about the screen being on."

Olivia picked up the disk. "This'll tell us, unless his Mac's different from mine."

Minutes later they had precise dates and times. The first entry had been saved at 4:23 on the Saturday of the wedding, the final entry at 9:58 on the night of the murder.

"And Lori found him around eleven-thirty," said Olivia.

"She says. Besides, an hour and a half isn't exactly a pinpoint of opportunity. Let's read."

In Olivia's case, this was easier said than done. Her exposure to pornography had been slight. Not her thing, nor Philip's; standard movies, fiction, works of art having been stimulus enough. The Greek and Roman sculpture in the Vatican Museum, for instance, had sent them tearing back to their *letto matrimoniale* for relief.

But more than a lack of familiarity with the genre complicated Olivia's search for insight, clues, or whatever she and Dee were doing. There was the whole distraction of having known the author, constantly hearing, in exchanges of dialogue, Rob's nasal, arch voice. And, just as Lori had predicted, each escalation of dominance and submission seemed linked to Lori's domestic torments.

Not to mention the whole weirdness of reading this stuff with Dee. Long as she'd known him, as freely and easily their talk had ranged over an enormous variety of subjects, they'd fenced off sex, tacitly and mutually left it alone. Maybe because he was gay, probably not because she was a woman. He hadn't talked sex with Philip, either.

He was getting way ahead of her. She'd better focus.

Rob stood, feet apart, implacable. Tracing the edges of his clean white briefs was a delicate tan line.

K's eyes clouded with desire and longing as she knelt in supplication before him. "Please," she begged. "Oh, please."

Her soft, open lips were only inches from his pouched sex. Feeling himself begin to harden, he stepped back, tightening his hold on the whip. Expertly he sent its lithe leather stinging across her full white breasts. Her cry was sharp, involuntary. Two quick flicks of his wrist gave each nipple a harsh kiss.

Comprehending the entirety of her helplessness, accepting and embracing it, she gave a low, hungry moan. "I'm yours," she told him. "Without you I'm nothing. Give me what I need and I'll be whatever you want."

His cruel smile softened. A delicious sense of power and fulfillment coursed through him.

Olivia had to take a breather. For all her distaste, she had to admit the power of these passages to arouse. Not the pain, of course—she hoped that taste would never be hers—but the woman's submissiveness. Into her mind jumped Lori's bent neck, her white scalp under the sink spray. And she wondered: Had Lori, too, found Rob's writing sexy, in spite of her sufferings at his hands, in spite of everything? Never in a million years would Olivia ask. Submission as turn-on: She could scarcely confess it to herself, much less to another.

Dee leaned over, interested to see where she'd halted. "You noticed that too, huh?"

"What?"

" 'Give me what I need and I'll be whatever you want.' Strikes a false note. 'K' hasn't been that articulate."

"Not nearly." Good. They were going to have a nice literary discussion. "What's it mean, that kind of mistake?"

Dee shrugged. "If we're sure this is a first draft, it's most likely simple carelessness."

"Is Rob's novel anything like this?"

"Good question. The compression's similar—and surprising to find in this context. Your average pornographer gets paid by the word, so why use one where four or five will do? Aside from that, I don't see much comparison. These are just sketches. K arrives at Rob's house, he starts doing something to her he hasn't tried before, she resists a bit, ends up loving it and begging for more. 'No,' says Rob, 'you've had enough,' and he shoves her out into the night. There's no narrative growth, no character development—none of what *Perfectly Honest* is loaded with. This isn't a developing story so much as a bunch of beads, same color, same size, same everything, strung on the usual flimsy cord."

"But each bead involves more pain than the one before. More danger."

"That's the formula. Death as ultimate rush."

"Oh."

"How do I express this? Lust festers into self-loathing and ends in violence. It accepts only two outcomes: self-destruction or the destruction of the object."

"Does this have anything to do with the Marquis de Sade?"

"Oh, honey. Whatever does it *not*? Why?"

"Rob, the real Rob, had a new-looking biography of him next to his reading chair. And an old paperback of *The Shelter-*

ing Sky, which I remember you telling me was better than the movie."

Dee, scholarly, pursed his lips. "Did I say that? I'm not a fan of either version. The novel goes over the top and the movie was too tame. But could Paul Bowles serve as a model for Rob's effort? It's possible."

Dee could go on in this vein for hours. Olivia tried something different. "You know how you always say fiction writers drop the ball when they use incidents from real life?"

"It's already real to them, so they neglect to make it real on the page."

"Maybe that's why the real Rob didn't catch the false note in 'Give me what I need and I'll be whatever you want.' "

"Because it's the real-life dynamic between him and the real K? I'm ready to call her Kim, by the way."

"Me too," said Olivia. "What might Kim need that Rob can give?

"This," Dee said, giving the manuscript a whack. "Debasement and its attendant ecstasies."

"Oh."

"You don't believe me? Real folks can't possibly carry on like this, groove on pain?

"I read the daily paper; you won't catch me predicting what real folks will or won't do. And spare me your latest on the human animal as evolutionary error, okay? It's been a morning from hell. I don't have the strength for failed monkeys."

He laughed and they returned to their reading.

"Oh *no*," she cried.

"Yeah," said Dee. "I debated warning you."

Rob's plot had thickened. Kim had a sister, Ashley, eleven years old. The child doted on her. Would follow her anywhere, do whatever she asked.

Olivia reached for the next page, read briefly, dropped it as if scalded. "That's it. I'm done."

"It's basically predictable. Given *Perfectly Honest*, given him, given the conventions of the genre. Pure Sade, really."

Once again, thought Olivia, professional distance rides to the rescue. Lucky Dee, able to cast ghastly cruelties into literary terms.

Before she could say anything, the phone rang. She looked at her watch. Almost two. The press conference would be well under way or over, and she'd forgotten to reinstall her normal message. Too bad. She couldn't possibly pick up and explain. Ashley's fate had left her in no condition to talk to a normal human being.

James Warriner's voice came over the speaker. Sounding very businesslike, he asked Olivia to call him as soon as she could.

14

Iames Warriner, boy DA?" breathed Dee.

Olivia nodded, hardly liking this reference to James's relative youth.

"Are you *sure* we don't have to volunteer information?"

"He's a friend," Olivia said stiffly. "We're having dinner tomorrow."

"Well, shut mah mouf. Natural mistake, though. He didn't *sound* friendly. Oh, Lord. Oh *damn*, Olivia."

She had burst into tears.

Saying how sorry he was, what an idiot he was, he put his arms around her, held her until the long-pent river ran dry.

She blew her nose, listened to Dee apologize some more, told him again it wasn't his fault. She'd simply mislaid, in this day's tumult, a complication that threatened the bridge they'd built over Lori's morass.

James was Law. James was Politics. This was his first high-profile murder as DA. At the Kasarjians', brandy and coffee having given the conversation a bloodthirsty turn, he had touched on why so many big-city homicides go unsolved. "When cases do get closed," he'd said, "it's almost always because we were able to amass a great deal of solid information, eyewitness and otherwise, in the first forty-eight hours. Every subsequent day's delay lessens the hope of a solution."

Olivia, this very moment, was slowing things down, lessening the hope of a solution—a solution that would silence the critics who claimed James lacked the toughness and experience to be an effective prosecutor.

Obvious as this now seemed to her, she had managed to forget Law and Politics so completely that when she'd heard James's voice, her connections ran straight to sex, and sex alone. As she'd plowed through the loathsome diary, he, or at least a powerful idea of him, had been in the wings. (The first plausible man of her widowhood, where else would he be?) The trick was to keep one corner of your brain busily categorizing and filing: okay to remember; best forget; *great* to remember; bury deep and never dare remember.

Ashley, of course, had slammed the filing system shut. Even so, James's voice had sent her straight to sex. Failed-monkey behavior. Instincts and animal greed.

She blew her nose again. "I better call him. Wait. Are there entries for last Friday and Saturday?"

"Yes. I've already read them."

"What happens?"

Dee retrieved pages, scanned briefly. "Friday's pretty routine. Saturday's different. Kim ends up tied to the bed instead of her usual banishment into the night. She's all jangly because he kept working her up and refusing her the final glories of his blah blah blah . . . Here we are:"

> Rob stood close to the bed, gazing pensively down upon his anguished captive. He felt nothing, absolutely nothing. Whatever he did next would be merely cerebral, willed, devoid of passion.
>
> With an idle, almost regretful finger, he drew a line across her wrist. Her involuntary struggles against

her bonds had left the smooth white flesh savagely abraded.

"I could kill you myself," he dreamily proposed.

"Instead of making Ashley do it, he means," Dee explained. "You okay?"

"Barely. Is that the end?"

"Almost. I gotta say it, Saturday's prose is *not* up to standard. Cliché city."

"Yes," she beseeched him, "yes. Oh, please."

A strange emotion burst from his heart, blurring his handsome features. "But my darling, don't you understand? You'll be released, you'll be free. But what of me? I'll be left behind—with nothing."

"Ashley," she reminded him with grave gentleness. "You will have Ashley."

His smile was infinitely wise. "Another turn around the park? Ah, but what comes after? Yes. You begin to understand. The circle will close. Ashley will be lying as you are lying now, and I will touch her poor wrist." He broke off, drew his thumbnail sharply across the injured flesh.

K gasped at the pain, her eyes akindle with un-slaked desire.

"I will touch her thus. And come face-to-face, yet again, with my own bondage. My bondage to my—"

"Then he breaks into caps," Dee said. "Notes to himself, looks like."

MY WHAT?
SELF?
OH, COME. LA BITCHOLA WILL EXPECT BETTER THAN THAT!

"Who's La Bitchola?" wondered Olivia.

"I don't know. Look, it's only a few pages longer. Tell me why you asked about Friday and Saturday, and I can spare you the blow-by-blow."

"James walked me home from the Kasarjians'. We ran into Rob and Kim. Rob was high on something. Or drunk. He ragged James about looking like JFK. Kim asked Rob who JFK was. Rob howled with laughter and called her a national treasure. This was actually our second meeting—I didn't spell it out for Lori because she was already angry enough. The time Rob introduced me was the day after the diary starts. Listen, this thing belongs in the hands of a shrink. A what-d'ya-call, forensic psychologist."

"Warriner actually saw Kim?"

"I marched him out of there, but yes, he saw her."

"So maybe he called you about her. They always want to question girlfriends."

"What do I tell him about her? And the rest of it? Half of me wants to spill everything, skip town till someone's in jail. But where does that leave Lori?"

"Hard to say. Think she might be forced to *lie*?"

"I can't just sell her out. I was the one who insisted she couldn't go home to Rob."

Dee gave the manuscript a comprehensive wave. "The case could be made that you saved her life. The case could also be made that she's done little since but shoot herself in the foot."

Olivia clapped her hands over her ears and screamed.

It took Dee only a few minutes to reach the last page. Frowning, he went back, read through the past week's entries again.

"Who's La Bitchola?" Olivia asked again.

"Doesn't say. Could be Kim, but my gut feeling is she's external—his editor, his agent. Ask Lori if they're women."

"Could it be Lori?"

"Probably not. Has to be someone he needs to impress. You

know what's really striking about these last entries? The plug's been yanked on the dramatic tension. Things happen, but the dialogue's stilted and the action's mechanical. Well, porn's inevitably mechanical, but in the beginning it was less obvious. He even forgets to say how K got untied. Monday begins with her bringing Ashley to the house. The sisters pose in costumes—there's one of those rooting-through-the-old-trunk scenes, incredibly dull and hackneyed, videotaped by 'Rob.' Tuesday is nude posing, and Wednesday is sister-on-sister defilement. Everything very trite and flabby. One thing we do ask of porn is *energy*. And, of course, videotape, photography of any kind, is greatly overused."

"It is?"

"Sure. You reduce the human body to two dimensions, you vastly expand its pornographic, that is, mechanistic, capability. Not in this case, though. Rob, the author, not the character, doesn't even have the kid separating herself and her feelings from her image and its antics, which *I* certainly would have explored. You look glum, chum. None of this helps you?"

"Will it help Law and Politics, is the question."

"The *core* question, if I may, is: Will the possibility of helping Warriner outweigh the certainty that Lori will go ape?"

"No. It's more like: Do I protect Lori or expose her to spare Lyman House an upset it probably can't survive?"

"Lyman House offers the greatest good for the greatest number." Dee was only musing, not insisting.

"The diary's embarrassing to Lori, not fatal," said Olivia. "And if she's really innocent, how can the police hurt her?"

"Being as her dear friend Olivia is cozy with the DA, maybe they won't. Unless Warriner's the kind who overcompensates in order to avoid, as they say, the appearance of impropriety. In which case he may urge the police to overcompensate too. Sorry. We Latino gays have to keep that sort of thing in mind. Also, who says she's innocent?"

"I can't stand this round-and-round. I have no idea what

kind James is—I just met the guy. I do know that the longer he waits for me to call back, the worse I'll look if Lori's blown."

"Yes. I'll leave."

"The one person I can trust in this infernal mess? I'm holding the receiver so you can hear. Don't miss a single nuance."

She was put right through.

"I wanted to call much earlier," James said, "but I was stuck in meetings. Are you all right? This must be awfully hard for you. The shock alone."

"We're okay, on the whole. Thanks for asking."

"Will you let me know if I can help in any way? That's me as new friend talking, but if you've got a minute, the DA has a question. Good. We're trying to find Rob Mallory's girlfriend."

"Her name's Kim Amundsen. Like the explorer, Rob said, which I guess is why it stuck. Thank 'Masterpiece Theatre.' "

"I'll send GBH a check today. Any more on her? Where she lives, works, anything?"

"No. Sorry."

"Not at all. The name alone puts you right at the top of the helping-hands list."

Olivia winced. "Are the cops asking the neighborhood about Kim? Good, because don't forget, both times I saw Rob with her, I was basically trying to squelch him. Other people might have stopped to talk, found out more."

"I hope you're right. So far we've only got two reports from witnesses who've seen her. Glimpses, like mine the other night. No conversations."

Initiative time. "I have a good visual memory. If a police sketch is in the works, I can probably help."

"Wonderful. Right now there are some legal constraints, but if we go that route, someone'll certainly call you."

"Say if I'm trespassing, but why so much interest in Kim?"

"Primarily because she hasn't come forth. She might be out

of town, of course, or unavailable for some other reason that has nothing to do with Mallory. But with homicide, we always want to talk to everyone close to the victim. Also, and this'll be in the news soon, the stabbing pattern indicates a crime of passion."

"You can tell that?"

"There's a neck wound that would have killed him instantly, which goes a long way toward explaining why no one heard a fight. Then the killer kept stabbing."

Until passion was spent. The primitive rages of girlhood helped Olivia understand. First you shove your little brother to the ground. Then you straddle his howling body and punch and sock until the fury that started the fight is spent. Then a final punch or two just because you can, just for the hell of it. "I can believe in a woman angry enough to kill that way, but would she be strong enough?"

"She'd have to know where to cut the neck, but that's street knowledge. The carotid artery gets lots of play on TV—though probably not during 'Masterpiece Theatre.' The other wounds are shallow in the chest, much deeper in the gut. The rib cage has a discouraging effect. So yes, a woman. Or a man who's not particularly strong. Either way, we don't think it's an experienced knife fighter. You'll probably be reading about the angle of attack, which indicates hatchet-style chopping. What an amateur would do."

A silence. Olivia didn't trust herself to break it. "Enough of that," James said. "More than enough. Are we still on for tomorrow night?"

"Are we? I mean, I hope so, but can you get away?"

"All work and no play makes a dull DA, and dull DAs don't close cases. But John Joseph Finn, my esteemed predecessor, gave me some good advice: Never eat out when the public's caught up in a juicy case. Time was, you could join me at the Salisbury Club, the one place in town we could count on being left in peace. However, my entry into politics has obliged me to resign from that august racist, sexist, elitist institution. Leaving us with a problem. And I do mean us, because we're a twofer— not only the head lawman but the new widow's close friend. We'll be irresistible."

"Not *close*," Olivia risked clarifying. "I feel for her. Anyone would. She's gone through hell."

"I think I hear a fine distinction. But does rampant public curiosity brake for fine distinctions? I'm afraid we've got only two choices—eat in or not at all. Not at all seems harsh, at least to me. So why not come to my place? I can promise the world's largest library of take-out menus."

"Sure. Or you could come here." But of course he couldn't. What would she do with Lori?

"When the storm and fury's over, I'd love to," he gracefully parried. "Tomorrow around eight? I'll send a cab for you. And, Olivia? You'll take care, won't you? Keep your street smarts cranked way up? Don't let anyone in the house without serious ID and don't go out alone. Not to sound paranoid, but a murder practically within earshot of the State House cops, God knows what we're dealing with. Better safe than sorry. Also . . . you're sure you're all right at home? With Ms. Lutz?"

"Yes," said Olivia. "By the way, no particular reason, but I haven't mentioned meeting you. Seems simplest to leave it at that."

"Indeed it does. See you tomorrow. I'm looking forward to it."

"Me too," said Olivia. She hung up and, moaning, buried her face in the sofa cushions.

"Relax," said Dee. "You did fine. Great move, offering to help with the sketch. And look at the goodies you got. Crime of passion! Well within the strength of a woman! An amateur!" He broke off, puzzled. "What's wrong?"

"Crime of passion; we can't possibly sit on the diary."

Dee thought about it. "He sounds okay, your Warriner. On the smooth side, but fundamentally okay. Maybe you should consider trusting him. And consider *not* trusting Lori."

"Don't warn her I'm handing over the diary?"

"Right. At least not until she's back in her own house and you've changed the locks here."

"I hate this."

Dee picked up the disk. "I'll print this for you. Just in case you decide Warriner should have it."

"I've decided. Copy the disk, too. I'll mail it to Mary Jane for safekeeping."

"With a letter to be opened in the event of trouble."

Yes, thought Olivia. Everything Lori's said that makes me think she's not the killer could be a lie.

Late that afternoon Lori called. Identifying Rob had knocked her for a loop, she said, but the press conference had been all right. No hard questions. "I spoke to Boy right afterwards," she said. "Planted the first seeds."

"How'd that go?"

"Well, you know Boy. He didn't exactly take in what I was saying. You guys enjoy your reading?"

"We didn't do it to enjoy it. Tell me something: Is Rob's agent a woman? Or his editor?"

"Rob work with a woman? You've got to be kidding. Why?"

"La Bitchola."

"Yeah. Weird. Not that the rest is anything but. I hope you guys aren't . . . Well, we went through that before. Listen, I really called to invite you to Felicity's loft. We've got a bunch of portable TVs, so we can compare each station's coverage."

Olivia declined, claiming exhaustion.

Dee had made lentil soup for supper and thawed one of his precious loaves of sourdough bread, supplied by a visiting friend from San Francisco. Olivia went down to his apartment in time to catch Lori's act on Channel 6.

The camera panned Mount Vernon's graceful brick house-fronts, then came in tight on the Lutz/Mallory rhododen-drons, leaves shiny with rain. Yellow police tape for background, the reporter summarized the murder and gave a capsule version of both Rob's and Lori's literary careers, with emphasis on Lori's financial success.

Cut to Lori, seated at a table, microphones clustered.

"That white shirt shows off the sling," Dee observed.

"Felicity's idea, Lori said."

"Rob Mallory was truly talented," Lori said, "and an abusive husband. I left him because I feared for my life, but I still loved him and I always will." Close-up on quivering lip, struggle for composure. "However he treated me, he never deserved this."

Cut to the studio and the next story. Olivia pressed the mute button.

"If it turns out she did it," said Dee, "that last line will get lots of play."

Reviewing the day before she slept, Olivia counted precisely three redeeming features. Dee was back by her side, James had been impeccable, and not one single person, acquaintance or friend, had called in hopes of inside info on Lori or the murder.

Pretty damned civilized. She might never satirize starchy Boston propriety again.

15

Friday morning Olivia learned from Mikey that "the condo people" were solidly behind the random-violence theory. "Which means," he said, "they accept it could happen again, you follow? Right here on exclusive Beacon Hill. To themselves or a loved one. Not so hot, right? But neither's the other side. They vote not-random, it's gotta be personal. They gotta face facts that a guy who looks and talks a lot like them, went to Harvard, wrote books, has a big house, the whole nine yards, can get himself up close and personal with a vicious killer. Then they gotta think: How many people who're up close and personal with *them* basically hate their guts? They count, and when they run out of fingers, they hafta vote random. The devil they don't know over the devil they do."

One of the more senior regulars was stirred to speech. "I say check out the homeless."

Mikey was scornful. "What, some crazy old stumblebum? Sleeps in the Commons he's lucky? He's gonna pull up his socks and stalk—"

"Who says stalk? I never heard 'stalk.' "

"Stands to reason," Mikey insisted. "Look at your foot traffic. Your dog walkers, your boys seeing their girls home—"

"Boys seeing boys home."

Laughter.

"They nail a homeless, you can say good-bye to that shelter."

"Residence, they're calling it now. But don't count your chickens. Your homeless, he's a victim of this society, right? So society, that's you and me, Jack, gotta improve his condition. We gotta take steps, do right by these misfortunate souls."

"We gotta make *amends*. It's *incumbent* on us."

Laughter.

"Just tell me one thing. When did they change it from 'bum' to 'homeless'? Huh? When was that? Who decided?"

Mikey gave Olivia her change. "What about you, Mrs. Chapman? You voting random?"

"I'm not sure."

"And her? The wife?"

The Spa held its breath. "Did you see her on the news last night?" Olivia asked.

"Yeah, but what's she say when it's just the two of you?"

"Nothing different," said Olivia, moving toward the door.

"Two women under one roof, that's all the talking they do? Quick, call the *Guinness Book of Records.*"

Olivia—see what a good sport I am?—laughed with the rest.

James's apartment was the top floor of a glorious late-Victorian pile, sunny side of Commonwealth. There was an elevator. Typical Back Bay, sniffed Olivia. Effete flatlanders. Won't climb anything but a StairMaster.

In her shoulder bag was the copy Dee had made of the diary. She planned (intended? hoped?) to hand it over to Law and Politics before she went home tonight. Her working assumption: The ideal moment for transfer, if and when it came, would be unmistakable.

It was the kind of elevator that opened right into your apartment. James, dressed exactly as she was, in jeans, flannel shirt, and Shetland sweater, took her coat; she took in the clean bare room. Beige wall-to-wall, two beige sofas facing each other, a glass-topped coffee table between. Heaped on it, the promised wealth of take-out menus. An unused fireplace was flanked by bookcases, empty except for a jumble of silver cups and bowls and a failing philodendron. On the floor next to the shelves were ranks of boxes, presumably filled with books.

She reviewed the evidence: Unpacks, but does not arrange, athletic trophies; does not unpack books; can't make the world's most durable plant thrive.

"White walls," said James.

Evidence on the credit side: Olivia loved it when people picked up on prior conversations. His abashed demeanor was neither a plus nor a minus. The decorator had run into it several times before, with other men recently divorced or transferred. I've been incredibly busy, it meant. And please don't ask if my busyness makes me so happy I like living in what might as well be a motel room.

A motel room with a grace note: three barrel-arched dormers fronting on Commonwealth. "Wonderful moldings," Olivia said.

"That's all the developer spared up here. The apartments on the lower floors have more detailing, but no view over the treetops. Come see."

Together they regarded the light-spangled city towers, the dark masses of branches nearly bare of leaves. Not as spectacular as Steven Dunbar's sweep of river viewed from Jacuzzi level, but romantic nonetheless, elegantly urban.

"The elms sold me on this place," James said. "I'd recently discovered why so many giant oldies have survived along here—it was the crusade of one Back Bay woman, Stella Trafford. She raised money to fight Dutch elm disease, prodded the city to prune and plant replacement trees, got volunteers interested. So now, whenever bureaucratic clog starts weighing me down, here's this terrific corrective, right in my face. The power of the individual citizen."

He was dead serious, Olivia saw. Good. She liked a politician to respect the power of the people who paid his salary. But with politicians you attend to what they do, not what they say. Elms, schmelms, that philodendron was dying.

"Something to drink," he proposed. "I've got the usual hard stuff, red and white wine, and beer of many stripes—lite, non-alcoholic, normal, and dark."

"White wine. And, not to preempt, can we consider food? I'm starving."

"Me too," he said, and indicated the menus. "Take a look while I get our wine."

Olivia pushed for Thai, Abbott's call having set up a hankering she'd had no opportunity to satisfy until now. "Unless you hate it?"

"I'm an omnivore. Except for flame-thrower spicy."

Olivia volunteered to phone the order in. Beef and chicken satays, extra peanut sauce, pad thai, shrimp in coconut milk, broccoli with ginger, ginger ice cream if they'd swear delivery unmelted.

"I'm glad you asked for extra peanut sauce," James said.

"I've been known to blob peanut butter on my salad plate the way normal people blob Brie."

"How do you feel about grilled cheddar-cheese-and-peanut-butter sandwiches?"

"Heaven."

"Reese's cups?"

"Stop. I'll have an attack."

"Sit tight, I'll only be a minute."

While he was out of the room she cased the trophies. They were all for squash, played at Groton, Harvard, and the Salisbury Club he'd had to resign from. The engraved dates gave her his age: thirty-seven or -eight.

Young but not too young. Whatever she meant by that. Not embarrassingly young?

She hoped he wasn't rummaging for Reese's cups. This hungry, starting with candy would give her a stomachache.

"*Et voilà.*"

On his tray were a bowl of carrot sticks, two napkins, two butter knives, and a jar of Smucker's peanut butter, properly stirred. "I used to mix it with mayo," he said, "for dipping. But this is healthier."

"Much healthier," said Olivia, troweling away. She took a bite. The carrots had been very fresh to begin with, then crisped in water in the refrigerator. "Brilliant," she pronounced.

He beamed. "My new secret vice. You're the first to know."

Years of smiling back at handsome men saved her. He'd never guess that his flirtatious reference to secret vices had flung her into the open sewer of the diary, muck about to close over her head.

Just in time, the doorbell. Chow coming up.

"Politics," she said when the edge was off her hunger. "How did you get started?"

"I worked on a campaign when I was in college. Took to it right away. You learn a lot, campaigning. More than in most classrooms."

"Were these presidential campaigns?"

He laughed. "I was wondering when we'd address the *R* word. I was a Young Republican for Carter. Reagan aged me fast, and I nearly bolted. I never had much hope for Bush, but by then the Massachusetts Miracle was bankrupt. Locally, the Republicans were the ones with the creative ideas. I'm glad I hung in. I will now pause for your scheduled rebuttal."

"No rebuttal. I vote the person, not the party. I don't really understand party loyalty. My image of it is people in funny hats waving placards and screaming."

"To me, politics, party or otherwise, is only the price of admission. Not the show."

"What's the show?"

"Serving the public good." He speared the last piece of broccoli. "Feel free to snicker."

"What's to snicker?"

"Countless scoundrels have appointed themselves guardians of the public good."

"You didn't sound scoundrelly when you defended Boy Lyman's residence." He seemed not to understand. "At the Kasarjians'," she prompted.

"Oh, right."

Olivia tried not to pounce. "Do you still think the residence is a worthy idea?"

"Sure." He smiled, onto her. "I drew a blank because that project came up in a different context today. Several heavy contributors who live near Boy called the governor. They wanted him to know that murder is inevitable once you start introducing alien elements into long-established neighborhoods."

They nail a homeless, you can say good-bye to that shelter.

"I've been congratulating us," James continued, "for not talking about our case."

"Yes. We're admirable."

"This food's pretty good, isn't it? Have some more. Sure? Ice cream, then. They really load the candied ginger, and it's worth every calorie."

Along with dessert, James's personal history. "Kitsy fell in love with another man and wanted a divorce. It hurt my feelings some and my ego immensely, but I found myself unable to sustain much of a fight. *Why* became clear when her romance fizzled and she wanted to reconcile. I said No thanks, which means I'm now the villain of the piece."

There was a daughter, thirteen. "Cammie shops. Endlessly and without discernible enjoyment. Let me ask you something. When you see your husband in your kids, do you like what you see?"

"Usually. Fractionally more than when I see myself in them."

"Yeah. I envy you."

"Poor Cammie."

"I know, I know. I drag her to museums, Symphony, other places she hates, and tell myself it's a stage, she'll outgrow it."

"That's valid. Thirteen-year-olds are the lifeblood of the American mall."

"What are your kids like?"

"Abbott's the one with the Thai girlfriend. He's an honor student, a bit of a loner, emotionally reserved. I hope it's just reserve. Ryland lets it all hang out. Works not very hard for Cs. He's a good athlete, but this term he switched to theater. He must be good at that, too—they gave him Nanki-Poo."

"My God. I was the Mikado."

As would any other man blessed with this history, he burst irrepressibly into song.

My object all sublime, I shall achieve in time,
To let the punishment fit the crime,
The punishment fit the crime.

"Obviously you were destined for the District Attorney's Office," said Olivia. Pitching the melody for alto comfort, she finished the verse.

And make each pris'ner pent, unwillingly represent
A source of innocent merriment,
Of innocent merriment.

"I was Peep-Bo," she explained.

They grinned at each other like idiots and moved to *Iolanthe* and *Pinafore*, then on to Broadway show tunes, sixties pop and folk, ancient campfire numbers. After a while, a refinement: each new song bite had to have some connection to the one previous. Irving Berlin's "Lazy" led to "Up a Lazy River" to "Proud Mary" to "Shenandoah" to "Cry Me a River" to "It's My Party." Leslie Gore's anthem to teen angst stumping James, Olivia was allowed to pick the next theme. "My Blue Heaven" led to "Blue Velvet" to "Blue Moon" to "Carolina Moon" to "Chattanooga Choo Choo" to "City of New Orleans," and on and on.

Until Olivia looked at her watch and was shocked. The lateness of the hour, though, was nothing compared to the jolting dissonance between all this . . . this innocent merriment and the diary.

"Should I call a cab?" James asked.

Or kiss you? he was really wondering.

She let his silent wish draw her toward him. As if final proof of his trustworthiness would radiate from the taste and feel of his mouth, the smell of his skin and hair.

"I have to stop," she told him at length.

"Mmmph. Don't want to."

Well, of course he didn't. What red-blooded woman would have it otherwise? But she pulled away. Had to. Had to sit all alone in her corner of the sofa, hot face burning, and ask the DA whether Rob Mallory's murder was still being considered a crime of passion. Then, no exit, she had to declare herself ready to snitch.

He was not one of those men who can turn on a dime, she was glad to see. It took Lori's discovery of Rob's body to banish the lover and place the lawman in charge, ask about times, whether the body had been cold or warm.

Much as Olivia tried to play down Lori's lying, when James learned the truth about her sprain it was obvious that Willa

Keaton interested him more as corroborating witness than blackmailer. Whatever else Lori had or hadn't done, she'd been seen leaving that house; there was little reason to imagine the diary as anything but legit.

He leaned toward her, gave her hot face a brief caress. "This is rough on you. Different loyalties wherever you turn."

"It's going to get rougher when Lori knows she's blown. Which I intend to tell her as soon as she's back in her own house. Don't look at me like that. It has to be me. It'd be grotesque for her to hear it secondhand. And since one tiny leak will wreck everything, I'm asking you to keep my snitching to yourself until she's back in her own house."

"Confidentiality's no problem, but I don't like the two of you under the same roof. You're assuming her innocence. I can't."

Olivia smiled nicely. "Then let her get back under her own roof. Make the cops hustle."

"I'll do what I can. When you do talk to her, make sure she understands that if she comes clean on her own, she'll really help herself. But no stalling, mulling things over. Time's too crucial in homicides."

"I know. I remember what you said at the Kasarjians'."

He hesitated, then came out with it. "I wish you wouldn't call yourself a snitch. It's ugly. And false. Inaccurate."

You paste an ugly label on yourself, it matters less if someone you're trying to trust throws you to the wolves. Nyah, nyah, beat you to it! "You're right," she said. "I'll stop."

She reached for her shoulder bag. "The diary's vile. Time pressures or not, I didn't hand it over right away because I wanted our evening unpolluted."

"I'm glad you waited."

She explained the concurrence of the diary's dating with real-time events and her supposition that K was Kim Amundsen. "The first time I saw Rob and Kim together I was sure they were lovers. The diary's tortures might be entirely invented, nothing to do with the two of them. Obviously I think otherwise. And when you told me Kim hadn't come forward . . ."

"You've done right. Exactly right."

"It doesn't feel right. It feels lousy. Look, I'm going to give you the diary anyway, but I need to ask: Does it have to become public information?"

"If it's as important as you think, it may be admitted as evidence. Assuming the case goes to trial."

"But that's months away. Lori can use that time to grow calluses. So will you promise to keep it under wraps until the trial? Can I tell her that?"

"You can tell her I'll do my best."

She thanked him and handed over the diary.

His gallant struggle to keep his eyes on her instead of gobbling down the first page made her smile. "The sooner my cab comes," she said, "the sooner you can get back to serving the public good."

"She's at your house now? That worries me. It worried me yesterday, and everything you've told me tonight makes it worse."

"I'll be fine. She's absolutely in the dark. You going to call that cab, or do I have to do every single solitary thing myself?"

16

Olivia's breakfast the next morning was interrupted by a phone call. "Mrs. Chapman? It's Mr. Luongo. I'd like to see you at ten."

The police artist. Olivia told him ten was fine and hung up.

Cloak-and-dagger terseness. James, last night, had been concerned that Lori might pick up an extension. "I won't call myself, but if you hear from Joe Luongo, you'll know the diary's moved me to consider Kim Amundsen a suspect. Unless Joe tells you otherwise, he'll meet with you at the precinct house."

Olivia finished her oatmeal, dressed, and sneaked down the stairs. She hadn't seen Lori last night and was in no hurry to face her today. Until her appointment, she'd hang out in the Athenaeum, catch up on the shelter mags.

Built in the early seventies, the exterior of the precinct house was less stridently ugly than the city's norm for that period. Inside, though, it reeked of cheapo expediency, every surface scarred by hard use. Despite the No Smoking signs, it also reeked of cigar smoke.

The officer escorting Olivia tugged open a final door, startling the man pushing from the other side. In his late twenties or early thirties, he wore blazer and slacks and what Dee called a striver shirt—wide blue and white stripes, white collar and cuffs. No tie. Deference to Saturday, Olivia supposed.

"You're Olivia Chapman," he said, sticking out his hand. "Peter Brink. I've seen you around the Hill. Horrible thing, this murder."

"Horrible," said Olivia, hating his preppy bray. If one of her sons started talking like that, she'd yank him out of school so fast the turbulence would rip off his laundry tags.

"Mrs. Chapman? Joe Luongo. Thanks again, Mr. Brink."

Brink gave Olivia a wink, citizen to citizen. "Good luck," he said.

Luongo was a big guy, bald on top and ample in the middle. Deferentially—he might be the chief of an advertising campaign, she his agency's prize client—he handed her a pencil drawing.

"Did this come from Mr. Brink?"

"And the other witness."

"The hair's not bad," Olivia said.

Luongo had a rich, easy laugh. "Sounds like this might take a while."

Lori, all smiles, was waiting for Olivia in the living room. "Guess what?"

"*Sweet Harmony* won the Pulitzer Prize."

"Next best. They finished with my house. I can move back anytime. I just called Felicity, and she's going to stay with me for a couple of days. You know, in case I get the creeps." Her cute-kid face. "I'd have asked you, but then I thought, No, Olivia's kind of overdue for some time alone."

Olivia produced a small, confessional laugh.

"So did you and Dee decide?" Lori could hardly be more offhand. "About the diary?"

"Not yet. Let's get you moved before we talk."

"You know what? I'm going to call it good news that you haven't decided. I mean, a day that starts with getting back a house you thought was gone forever, how bad can it end?"

The day had turned suddenly warm, filling the streets with neighbors doing Saturday errands, walking dogs, and socializing. Lori's move had witnesses and commentators galore.

Transport was by foot, Dee's offer of help saving Olivia the nuisance of getting her van out of the garage. Lori kept the pretense of her sprain by carrying only a light sack. Olivia and Dee would manage the rest. "I can actually imagine using this stuff again," Lori had marveled while packing her reference materials, notebooks, computer, and printer. "I've been remembering a lot lately. Whole paragraphs, you know? And some of it's not that bad, either."

Passing through the rhododendron jungle gave Olivia a shiver, and the police search had not improved the state of the living room.

"Cat," pronounced Dee, spilling his armful of recruitment literature in his haste to open a window. Bingo padded out from the kitchen, looking extremely well fed. Without so much as a meow or proprietary swipe at Lori's legs, he scampered up the stairs, posting himself at midpoint, right in everyone's way.

"Watch it," Lori warned Dee. "He bites."

"I could tell," said Dee.

"This is so *great*," Lori exclaimed when Olivia and Dee arrived with the last load. "I really don't know how to thank you."

Dreading what lay ahead, Olivia could hardly respond. If only Lori hadn't gone in that night, if only Willa hadn't seen her!

Lori laid it on thicker. "You're my lifesavers, the both of you. No, I mean it. I'd never have gotten through this without you."

"You're not exactly home free," said Dee, making for the living room. "Let's sit down, talk some turkey."

Lori's dismay showed how completely she'd anticipated reprieve. "Sure. Want tea or something? God knows what's in the fridge, but . . ."

No takers, she followed them into the catastrophe of greasy take-out containers, smeared glasses, and flung-about newspapers. Dee opened another window.

"I've got to get someone in to clean," said Lori. "Either of you know anyone good? And not too expensive?"

"There's no easy way to do this," Olivia said. "Last night I met with a man who's investigating Rob's murder. I told him everything I know and gave him a copy of the diary."

Lori sat stunned. Then hatred, hot, furious, clenched her features. "Figures," she spat. "Typical rich-girl goody-goody, running straight to the cops."

"He said he would do his best to keep the diary under wraps until the case goes to trial. If you don't talk about it, no one else will, either."

"Expect me to believe that?"

"This man gave his word, and I trust him. You also have some short-term leverage, because you can narrow down the time of the stabbing. The police will want you to keep those details secret until they can check out Kim Amundsen's alibi."

Sullenly: "They find her yet?"

"No. Tomorrow there'll be a sketch in the papers and on TV. Plus the usual distribution through the police networks."

Lori's eyes narrowed. "You sold me out for Boy, didn't you? Oh, sure you did, don't bother to lie. God, do I ever regret the day I told Michelle to hire you. It's like they say, no good deed goes unpunished."

Dee had to laugh. "On that note," he said, standing.

Olivia stood too. "I was advised to tell you that Detective McGuire is expecting you to call him at this number, the sooner the better."

Lori refusing the card she held out, Olivia laid it on a pizza lid. "You'll do as you please, but they said to tell you that you can help yourself enormously by volunteering a prompt, full statement of exactly what you did and saw on Wednesday night."

The front door banged open and Felicity came in, a heavy-looking duffel in each hand. Seeing Lori sunk in despair, she dropped her bags and turned on the others. "What have you done to her?"

A long silence. Lori pushed herself slowly out of her chair. Her voice gravelly, she asked Felicity to excuse her a minute, she had to make a call.

Dee and Olivia fled.

"Rough trade, too?" Dee murmured once they were on the sidewalk. "This case has *everything*."

"That's the leader of the gang who wrecked your writing session. Name's Felicity Starshine."

Glee. "Starshine?"

"Failing Kim, she's my favorite suspect."

"Oh, mine too. At first sight. Tell me more."

"While we're waiting for the locksmith," Olivia promised.

They walked fast, filling their lungs as if to purge the nastiness. Olivia identified a familiar feeling: a troublesome client's bill had been paid in full and the check hadn't bounced. On the heels of this, a realization dawned. *As long as she was in my house, I had to believe she was innocent. Now I don't.*

Failing Kim, her favorite suspect was Lori.

17

Two days later winter arrived, sleet mixed with snow, clearing cold enough to freeze the whole slushy mess treacherously solid. Thursday evening, Olivia bundled up and picked her way to Chestnut Street. The Lyman House board was holding its regular meeting. Boy had wanted Michelle, but she was in Washington, testifying at HUD. Olivia was second-best.

It would be her first encounter with Lori since the whistle-blowing. Kept current by James, Olivia knew that Kim Amundsen was still missing. Efforts to find an address, driver's license, any other trace, had led nowhere. Also, Lori had given McGuire the same story she'd told before, when prompted by Willa Keaton's blackmail. Did this mean it was true? Or only that Lori had managed to lie with unshakable consistency?

Olivia told herself to knock it off. Such questions were for the Law, not her. If her delivery of the diary, or help on the sketch, assisted the cause, fine. Essentially, though, the pros were on the job, and she was out of it.

Out of the muck and morass, that is, but enjoying a corksome float in clear fresh waters. Yesterday Val, Steven Dunbar's intended, had dropped by. No advance warning. Val's initial demeanor was bristling, defensive, but the decor of

Olivia's office settled her nicely. (Faux, Mission, and Deco are natural soulmates.) "I think I've bitten off more than I can chew," she began. Minutes later, Olivia was back on the job, her terms.

"Just like that?" Val asked. "No told-you-so?"

Olivia grinned. "Give a bride a hard time, you get seven years bad luck."

"Really? I never heard that before."

"I just made it up. But it might be true, so I won't say a word."

James, too, was part of the corksome float. He was a find, a gem, a darling. His phone briefings were conscientious, concerned, and, often as not, sexy at the finish. He was coming for dinner tomorrow. Baked oysters, she'd decided. Sexy at the finish.

The board meeting was in a small room off the drafty, echoing grand salon. Boy had set up a rudimentary office, using his new folding chairs and the old kitchen table, its printed oilcloth cover (skillets, potted geraniums) much scarred by cigarette burns. There was an ancient file cabinet and a small electric heater, its glowing element no match for the icy blasts rattling the windows.

Lori, talking hard to worshipful Boy—any closer and he'd be in her lap—didn't interrupt herself to greet Olivia. The others, Charlie Pierson, Becky Krebs, and Helen Rowantree, were so welcoming and nice that Olivia might as well have been Michelle.

Boy gave her a wave, causing Lori to turn, make a little drama of noticing Olivia for the first time. "Oh, hi," she said.

"Hi, Lori."

"How's life on the crest of Joy? That's what she calls her house," she amplified for the group. "It's a pun. Cute, huh?"

How on earth had Lori discovered Philip's private joke? Olivia pasted on a smile. "Everything's fine."

"Dee scribbling away?"

"He's in Belmont, actually. His mother's down with a bad flu."

"I wish Rob had family nearby. His brothers expect me to do the funeral totally on my own. And his mother! She basically told me she might have a better offer, but if those plans didn't jell, she'd consider showing up."

Charlie Pierson cleared his throat. "Well!" cried Becky Krebs with a purposeful clap of her hands. "We're all here, let's start."

Fund-raising occupied the first half of the meeting. Boy asked Olivia to restate her belief that the conservatory could be dismantled and profitably sold. Helen Rowantree gave a cry of protest. Like the ancient at the public meeting, she remembered the house in its glory days. Much back-and-forth followed, Helen eventually conceding that antique splendor must kneel to practicality when budgets were as tight as this one.

Why so tight? Neighborhood donors were not coming forth as numerously or generously as hoped. "It's this dratted murder," Charlie Pierson crossly complained. "People keep telling me life's already too dangerous, Beacon Hill simply can't absorb any more change."

Despite Lori's earlier complaints about Rob's funeral, the Grand Old Man had obviously forgotten her special relationship to the dratted murder. Olivia sneaked a look around the table. Everyone but Pierson was studying the skillets and geraniums on the oilcloth.

"We should move on," Boy suggested. "We need to make some decisions on the balance of public space to private. I know we've talked about the residents' inclination to isolate themselves, but I've been reading a précis of the president's task force on the homeless and . . ."

By the time they broke up, Olivia could think of little besides a long hot soak in the tub. Lori had ducked out early, giving no excuse. Poor Boy, surprised and disappointed, had gulped like a guppy.

Mindful of the ice, Olivia walked as fast as she dared. Running would be warmer but too hazardous, even with L.L. Bean's best boots. Turning onto Joy, the wind smacked her full in the face, stealing her breath, stinging and blinding her eyes. She was glad of the heavy cashmere shawl she'd wrapped twice around her head.

She pulled off a mitten, fished the icy keys from her pocket, fumbled them into the lock. Finicky, possibly frozen, it resisted turning. When at last she pushed the door into the little foyer, a small sob of relief broke from her. *Home.* Worth every one of the zillion pounds of gold, flesh, toil, and spirit it had cost and would continue to—

A rough push from behind, a shove that sent her slamming into the bench. Someone banged the door shut, slapped off the foyer light. Windows framed the door, but the illumination of the gaslit street barely penetrated. No one passing by would notice anything amiss, not that there'd be much foot traffic this bitter night.

Olivia's shins stung from hitting the bench. Low in her back, a painful jabbing.

"That feel like a gun? It should." A man's voice, low-pitched but nervous. Young. A smoker's sour breath. "Turn around and I'll blow your guts out. Scream and I'll blow them out twice. Drop your keys. Right. Take off that scarf and your parka and drop them. Now drop yourself. Facedown."

"Here? There's no room."

"Don't make me mad, okay? Head first." The gun jabbed toward the foyer's inner door, still locked.

Rape, she knew. Every woman's nightmare hour come round at last.

She had to lie at a slight angle, her head pressed against the inner door, her feet against the outer. He kicked at her to force her legs open, then jammed a heavy boot into her fork legs.

She cried aloud at the pain. "Shut up. The gun's right on you. Bring your hands around real slow and cross your wrists."

He wasn't going to rape her here, then. They were going inside. Into her private territory. A double defilement.

Keeping his boot hurtfully in place, he crouched. That medicinal smell had to be adhesive tape, strapping on good and tight. Too late she remembered that James Bond always clenched his wrists to make them big, gain leeway. She heard clinking. He'd picked up the keys.

He stood. "Upsy-daisy," he said, less nervous now. "Face the bench."

Not easy, getting up without hands. There was just enough light to see his position relative to hers. Delaying, pretending to be more stuck and helpless than she was, she flashed on a brawl she'd won instantly—one good kick to her older brother's balls. But the way this guy stood over her, the angle was hopeless. And the gun meant no second chance if she missed.

"Move it," he barked, booting her again.

She gasped, moved.

Gun against her back, he took two tries to find the right key. He asked was there a switch right inside the door and she said yes. Carefully he cracked the inner, windowless door, doused the stairwell lights, and prodded her inside.

When the lights were back on, she glanced down, saw that the torturing boots were Sorels. Klondike boots, expensive and faddish.

"We're going to the top floor," he said. "Just like normal."

He knew her habits. He'd been watching the house. Did he know Dee lived here?

As if to answer, he beat a mocking tattoo on Dee's door. "Your pet fag's missing all the fun."

"He's teaching karate down at the health club. Should be home any minute now."

"You wish. Too bad he's having a sleepover with Mommy."

Ice gripped her heart. Dee had decided to go to Belmont only last night, and then taken off for the Bentwood, a gay bar famous for oddballs and weirdos. "Laying down a good thick base," he'd explained, "for filial duty."

"Shit, more stairs? Hold it, I gotta catch my breath."

Dee *cultivated* weirdos. Claimed they were essential to his artistic vision. Familiarity with the strange, he'd say, gives a writer access to the strangeness within the familiar.

Chattering carelessly away, he'd exposed her to this. She thrust the horror of it away, fought for calm.

"You're rich, why no elevator?" the rapist grumbled.

"Let's go back down. To my office."

"So anyone on the street can hear you yell? Not a chance."

"I won't yell. I promise."

He laughed.

"Seriously. I've got two sons, vulnerable ages, both of them. Remember when you were in your teens? And their father's just died after a long—"

"Shut it. Too late for that shit. Way too late. Your own fucking fault. *Move.*"

Her fault? What was he talking about?

Ton of bricks, the answer hit. Lori. She'd told Lori that Dee was away, Lori had left the meeting early. One phone call to Mr. Sorels here and—

And what? Sweet revenge? A dose of real-world terror for the goody-goody, her trusted police nowhere to be found?

They reached the top floor. He kept her in front of him while he moved about, turning on lights. "Oh my," he gushed, vamping ladies' lunchspeak. "Isn't this lovely. Who's your decorator? No, let me guess. I bet you did it all by yourself, you clever little thing."

The phone rang. "Don't move," he warned her.

The machine picked up and they heard Dee's voice. "Just doing bed checks. Call when you get in. If I don't talk to a real human being soon, I'll die." He gave his mother's number and hung up.

"Who was that?"

"Dee." Doesn't know him well, she feverishly thought, didn't recognize his voice. "There was a murder near here. Everyone's pretty anxious. He'll keep calling until he gets me."

"Oh no, none of that. You're gonna call him."

"He wants to chat. How do I handle that with a gun in my back?"

"You got a boyfriend? What's his name? The fag know him too? Okay, you call back, say you just got in, James is with you and everything's cool. Nothing else, understand? What's the number?"

He punched it in, held the receiver to her ear.

"Hi, Dee," she said. "I just missed you. Look, I'd love to talk but James is here, so . . ."

"James?"

"Mm."

"Say no more. Call me tomorrow."

She said she would and hung up. The gun prodded. "Sit there."

He shoved her toward the side chair next to the fireplace. She could hardly be farther from the phone or the kitchen with its knives and gas burners. (In a movie—she saw the sequence in a single, vivid instant—she'd free her hands with flame. Distract the rapist somehow, turn the stove knob with her teeth.) Just to her left were the poker and other fireplace tools.

Behind her back, still unseen, he unzipped his parka, tossed it onto the sofa that faced the fireplace. Like his boots, the parka looked expensive. A privileged rapist. Dressed for the neighborhood, fit right in.

One by one, he pitched the fireplace tools in the direction of the staircase. The poker struck the china lamp next to the phone, knocked it to the floor. Smithereens. For God's sake, she told herself, don't start mourning *lamps*.

He took the armchair opposite her, Philip's favorite, and showed himself. Slim, her height or a bit under, late twenties. Blond, almost white hair, short at the sides, long on top. Blue eyes, pale lashes and brows. Handsome, if you like them with delicate features.

He switched on the drafting lamp that Philip had liked for reading. Tilted the shade so it shone uncomfortably in her eyes.

He was fairly close to her, about four feet of air separating their knees. The gun was aimed at her chest. Too close for a shot to miss, too far for her to attempt to kick the gun away, assuming she'd risk a move so dangerous. (How to distract him? That part of the movie remained a maddening blank.)

"Ta-da," he caroled. Here I am, fans, his free arm signed. Let's hear some *applause*.

Olivia stared, nonplussed by this goofy turn.

"Oh, come *on*." He tossed back his hair, gave her a three-quarter profile, a movie-star smile.

Squinting past the light, she had it. "Kim," she breathed.

Instantly he braced to shoot. "Call me that again, I'll kill you faster than him."

"What . . . what should I call you?"

"Brad. Brad Lund. Too close to Lutz, so he changed it."

"Fine, Brad. Sorry for the mistake. It won't happen again." That flowered scarf! It had been for his Adam's apple. But what had he done about his voice?

He held his aim a moment longer. Then he sank back into his chair, gun careless in his lap. "You know what I could go for? A nice frosty beer."

Struggling to collect her wits, she told him there was plenty in the refrigerator. She'd never heard him speak as Kim, she now realized. Not once.

He stood, warning her to stay exactly where she was. "I'm a fantastic shot. Deadeye Dick. Don't even turn around."

She sat as ordered. Think, she told herself. He's given you some time, use it. Forget rape, forget Lori. This is Rob and murder. But what had brought him here? The sketch? It wasn't all that accurate, she could see now. Besides, without the prompting of wig, makeup, clothing, who'd make the connection? Why not just stay missing forever?

Concentrate! Brad ambushed Rob, killed him on the spot. Ambushes you and you're still alive. Why?

Being called Kim had enraged him. Shame? Self-disgust? He didn't know she'd read the diary, of course. And he might not know it existed. How to use it? How to use that anger linked to Kim?

He was back in Philip's chair, gun trained on her, beer bottle in his free hand. He took a good swig, exhaled a *pah!* of satisfaction, set the bottle on the lamp table. Then he used his teeth to rip the cardboard off his book of matches, shook out a cigarette one-handed, bent a match and flicked it with his thumb. No candyass safety feature's gonna stop a tough guy from doing what he wants.

He smoked hungrily, swallowed more beer. "Your pet fag's brand? Yeah. I hate to say it, but the spics do good beer."

"Have you known Dee long?"

A scowl. "Long enough."

"He and my husband were college friends, and—"

"Yeah, yeah, I got the whole story from Rob. Guys like your husband made him puke."

"I don't understand."

"'Course not. Cunts never understand a thing. I oughta know—I've done enough of them. Give me a fag anyday. Leastways with fags a man knows where he *is*. They've got a sense of shame, you know? Cunts, no. It's okay at first, simple fee-for-service deal. Then it starts. 'How come you never call just to talk? How come you never send flowers? I'm letting you use my car, can't you at least open the door for me?' " He shook his head, disgusted. "Chinese water torture."

Olivia nodded as if in sympathy. "Demanding," she murmured.

"Believe it."

She had to keep him talking. Had to arouse in this cool young hustler an urgent conviction that she was the best, the only person on earth who would understand about him and Rob. "Can we go back to something you said before? About Rob and Philip?"

"Who's Philip?"

"My husband. You said guys like him made Rob puke."

"Account of he got away with it. The wife, the nice house, kids, good job, respect, the whole magillah—plus, anytime he wanted, fun with the pet fag. Foot in both worlds, right?"

Having smoked his cigarette down to the filter, he ground it into the ashtray and swigged more beer. "Don't you go thinking," he warned. "Nature calls, I'll piss right here. You want to, you can watch. I won't even charge you."

Intending only to gross her out, he'd handed her a thread, fearfully weak, to survival. "In case you change your mind," she said, "the bathroom's down one flight."

He answered this with an evil grin and busied himself with another cigarette. Three flicks this time. The striking surface must be wearing thin.

Infinitely more significant, though, was what he didn't do. He didn't look past her toward the curve of paneling in the corner of the room, didn't jeer, Listen, cunt, I've climbed enough stairs tonight. I want a bathroom, I'll use that one.

Meaning that the secret-chamber door to the lavatory wasn't wide open. Meaning, please God, she had left it slightly ajar, the way it was supposed to be in weather this cold.

So. On top of the diary, she knew something else Brad didn't. The lavatory wasn't sanctuary, hardly that, but a thread.

A hope. To grasp it, she must entice, cajole, seduce Brad into craving more and more of her listening ear. Make him talk on and on—long enough for something to change, convert the thread into a lifeline.

"You and Rob really had something special," she began. "That first time I saw you together? I'd just been to a wedding. The bride and groom were in love all right, but nothing like you two. I was really envious."

He seemed at once furious and hungry for more.

She chanced it. "He sure liked showing you off."

Deprecatory, mouth down at one corner: "Yeah, well. That was my first time out in public."

"But you looked so natural. Terrific, in fact."

He laughed harshly. "Save it. Think I'm some ditsy queen, wants to talk makeup and hairdos? The drag routine was for him, not me."

"For him," Olivia repeated encouragingly.

"I'm the only guy he ever made it with, you know. I walked into the Bentwood that night and he was like ka-*pow*."

"The Bentwood. I think I've heard Dee mention it."

"He spends enough time there," Brad said with one of his smiles. "Last night he went on and on about his poor sick mom."

A pause for her reaction. She gave him the shocked gasp, the wide-eyed dawn of recognition.

"Fags," he sneered. "Can't keep their mouths shut." He looked at her closely. "You're thinking, Why's he keep dumping on fags when he's one himself? Come on, admit it, that's what you're thinking."

"I'm not big on labels. People are too complicated."

"Anything goes, huh?"

"More like pigeons belong in pigeonholes, not people."

"Pigeons. Rob was always trying to kick them. He had this song about kicking pigeons in the park."

Olivia risked a probe. "Makes him seem a bit, I don't know . . ."

"Cruel? Vicious?"

Was this an opening for dialogue? Olivia wasn't sure, and a premature step in that direction could backfire. "Hard-hearted," she suggested. "Though hardly in the same league as beating up your wife."

Brad showed his disgust. "He belted her a few times. You call that cruel?"

"What do you call cruel?"

"You don't want to hear."

"Probably not."

Smoke time again. Flame on the fourth try. *"Probably not,"* he mimicked. "You forgot this." He aimed the gun. "I get to pick what we talk about."

Olivia had no trouble showing consternation. "Absolutely," she said.

"Try this for cruel. A guy wanders into a bar, gets into this serious rap, one-on-one, with one of the fags. The guy's all sensitive and worried, see. Doesn't understand what's been happening to him lately. He's started to feel this terrific attraction to men, the whole gay lifestyle. But he's got a wife, kids. Sex with the wife has dried up to zilch, but he still cares about her, and of course he loves his kids. Two boys. Great little troopers, Little League stars. 'I can't hurt them,' he goes, 'I just can't do it to them.' The fag, of course, takes the bait. He lays out the basic line—you only go around once, you have to be true to yourself, in the long run, you'll hurt your family more by living a lie.

"But the guy's all blushy and stammering, and then it's out—he's a total virgin. Never even been kissed. So of course the fag takes the rest of the bait. Promises he won't do anything the guy doesn't want, but how about going someplace quiet, talk, get to know each other."

Caught up in his story, Brad had leaned forward, tight focus on Olivia's face. Now, as if embarrassed by his intensity, he fell back with a mocking laugh.

"This isn't going to have a happy ending," said Olivia.

"Believe it. They go to the fag's place. The fag tries a starter kiss. Light little brush on the lips, maybe just the cheek. Whatever, the guy explodes, beats the fag to a bloody pulp."

Brad upended his beer, drained it, banged the empty on the table. "You call that cruel?"

Olivia didn't answer. Once she'd been sure he'd finish his story no matter what, she had started to wince, roll her shoulders, struggle to find a more comfortable position.

He peered at her. "Hello? Anyone home?"

"I'm sorry. What's the question again?"

"Jesus H! This guy I've been telling you about! You call him cruel?"

"Of course. Anyone would."

"Wrong. Most folks would say the fag got what he deserved. And nine times out of ten the fag would agree, account of the guy was such a good picker. He had like an instinct for marks who'd go boo-hoo-hoo, but I did the dirty, so what do I expect?"

"This is Rob you're talking about? He invented the kids and all?"

"Who else."

"How'd he keep getting away with it?"

"You think marks broadcast they've been suckered? Once he was dead, that's when things started coming out. I heard some of them formed a support group, can you stand it? DA, they should call themselves, Dumbfucks Anonymous. I'm getting another beer. Don't even think of moving."

Olivia could hardly think at all, she was so confused. Brad's brand of logic was too slippery for her. He kept undercutting her expectations.

When he returned with his beer she tried again to pin things down. "Was all this before he met you?"

"'Course it was. A, I'm no fag, and B, the reason I let him come on to me in the first place was I figured, What the hey, he's this famous writer, he can give me some tips."

She hunched her shoulders, let her face show pain. "Oh. You write too."

"What, you don't think a guy like me can write?"

"What gave you that idea? I was thinking you must have some incredible stories to tell."

"Believe it. Rob sure thought so. We didn't just fool around in the sack, you know. We were collaborators."

The diary. "You were writing something together?"

"Him, write? He could hardly stand to touch a pencil. Writer's block, they call it. I never had it myself, and from what he said, I gotta hope I never will. Wouldja stop that wiggling around? It's getting on my nerves."

She stifled a sob. "I *can't* stop. I've got bursitis in both shoulders. I've been trying to listen to you, pay attention to what you're saying, but it really *hurts*."

"Jesus, now she's bawling. Okay, look. I'll do your hands in front, but you try anything, you're dead meat."

He rummaged in his parka pocket for the tape, went to the kitchen for a paring knife. From behind her, he cut the tape with one hand while the other pressed the gun into the base of her skull. "Raise 'em high," he commanded.

As if arthritic, she cranked her arms around and up, whimpering in spite of herself, remembering James Bond when she crossed her wrists. She wiped her eyes on the cuffs of her sweater, let her hands drop slowly to her lap.

"Oh, that's so much better. Thanks. Really. So. You and Rob were collaborating on your novel?"

"Mostly on how to end it, because the rest is fine." He broke off, narrowed his eyes. "You got a problem with that?"

"Not at all. I'd like to hear more. Is it set in the present day?"

For once, a normal reaction: bravado mixed with shyness.

"Yeah. It's about this totally pure and innocent kid. Sweet face, blond curly hair, altar boy, the works. Then he gets raped by the priest. He works up the nerve to tell his mom and she's furious at him, calls him a liar, all that. Which of course makes the kid totally suicidal. He climbs this water tower and is about to jump when this angel appears, says it's not time. Tells him to go down and do the work he was created to do. So he does, and guess what happens in church next Sunday? The kid looks at the priest, and the priest gets this major hard-on. Right in front of the whole congregation. That's the power the angel gave him, see? The hard-on lasts until the kid looks away. After a while he's nailed every molester in the town—a teacher, a cop, and the president of the bank that's about to foreclose on his mom's house. It's comical, see. Not to the molester, but everyone else totally cracks up. Rob said the ending should be the kid follows this no-good presidential candidate around until his campaign's totally destroyed."

"I like it. He zaps the local bad guys and ends up saving the whole country. What's his name, by the way?"

"Ashley. I'm a *Gone with the Wind* freak."

Luckily he was occupied with striking a match and missed her reaction. The Ashley in the diary, K's sister, was to be forced by "Rob" to kill K. How to use this?

"Shit!"

The entire matchbook had caught. Reflex shook the flaring pack from Brad's hand to his lap, his panicky brushings sent it to the floor along with the gun.

A quick swoop and the gun was back in his hand, but the damage was done. No real gun ever hit like that. It was plastic. One of those convincing fakes, fool you even if you didn't have a light shining in your eyes.

Nada, nada, nada, she commanded herself as he stamped the matchbook. "You okay?" she asked. "You'll find more matches right next to you. In that brass thing."

Gun aimed, eyes fixed on her, he felt for the matches.

"Back to your novel," she said. "You know what I like best? The way Ashley can punish the molesters right on the spot. Suppose you'd gone the usual route, put them on trial and sent them to prison. Big deal. Parole and they're back in business before they're missed, right?"

He nodded, wanting more.

"But no one, presidential candidates on down, can survive ridicule. Hey! What did I say?"

Enraged, he'd braced the gun.

Olivia was the soul of kindness. "Rob handled his writing problems by ridiculing his wife's books. Did he make fun of yours?"

"It was you! Your fault! From the day you took that cow in, he was never the same. No matter what I did for him, the magic kept slipping away. La Bitchola, he called you. He was like, obsessed with you, what you were doing, what you were saying about him. Once he even made me pretend to be you. It really ate his guts that you picked her over him. Elsie the Cow over him! You sassed him and jerked him around and I took the brunt. Oh, *baby*, did I take it. The other night? When you were with that guy? Soon as we got inside the house I knew he was going to make me pay. But I don't convince easy, you know? I had to let him practically kill me, and then I had to listen to him wipe out the toilet with my novel."

Caught up in his hurt, desperately hungry for justification, for some response that would lift from him the entire burden of his anguish, he had drawn very close to Olivia. His knees were apart, the gun hanging loose as he leaned over his fore-arms. He seemed very young.

A spring of pity. Olivia squelched it instantly. He'd come boiling into her life, convinced she'd wrecked his romance. She was still alive for only one reason: He had learned a great truth in the aftermath of killing Rob. When murderous rage kills too abruptly, the entire burden of fury and grief is crushingly yours and yours alone until kingdom come.

She'd bet anything he had a knife strapped inside his boot. Sooner or later, he'd use it on her. He'd vented some of the fury and grief, but not enough, never enough. He'd realize that, and her use to him would evaporate. Besides, she knew he'd murdered; he'd have to cover himself. Didn't matter which motive dominated. Either way, she'd be just as dead.

"I'm afraid you're wrong about one thing," she said gently. "Rob was busily writing behind your back. He'd made a good start on a book, in fact. Lori found it in his computer and we both read it. Dee, too. Dee says it's the kind of sleaze that sells real well. He used the form of a diary. Mostly it's two characters, Rob and K, he calls them, involved in S & M games that get more and more dangerous. Dangerous for K, that is. Then Rob decides K should bring her little sister Ashley into the games. Yeah, that's what he called her all right. He forces Ashley to kill K, same as he tried to kill your novel. I wonder how much else he stole from what you two had together. I bet it was a lot. Your love for him, your whole life, really, as a man and a writer, turned into cheap porn."

Seeing him dazed, stunned past comprehension, she tensed, lunged upward. The full momentum of her body drove her fiercely clasped fists into the soft underside of his chin.

His head snapped back with a retching expulsion of air. His knees jerked up to protect gut and groin. Not from her, though. She was out of there, sprinting for the lavatory.

She opened the door enough to slip in, yanked it shut, slid the bar lock home. The screws ought to be good for at least one ramming, but best not count on even that. Grabbing the edge of the sink as well as she could, she twisted her body sideways and kicked out the window. Bless L.L. Bean, bless Bruce Lee. A corner shard looked sharp and steady. One hand inside, one out in the frigid cold, she began to saw herself free.

Expecting him to come thudding against the door at any moment, she didn't tumble at first to what she was actually hearing—male cries, heavy crashes. Then silence, baffling and ominous.

Sawing frantically, she was interrupted by a voice outside the door. "Olivia? Dee here. Our boy's resting quietly."

18

She opened the door. Dee had Ryland's baseball bat in one hand, an ugly-looking knife in the other. His left sleeve was torn and bloody. Brad, inert, lay by the fireplace.

Dee dismissed his injury. "It's a scratch, all he had left in him when I bonked him with the bat. What's he doing here?"

"He's Kim. He killed Rob. It's complicated."

"I'm sure. Did he tell you he knew me?"

"Yes. But Dee! What in the world made you come tonight?"

"First let's tie him up."

Brad still out and trussed with his own tape, Dee explained that the key factor had been his mother's addiction to all-news radio. "A reporter, a woman, was interviewing James right after a speech he'd made on gun control. Bullet control, really—tax ammo way out of sight, was the idea. The reporter asked him if he was afraid of the gun lobby. He said he wasn't, and she signed off live from Worcester. I called you right afterward to see if you'd gotten home from your meeting. You said James was on Joy Street. I hopped in Mom's car and broke all speed records. I was feeling a little alarmist until I saw your parka and scarf on the floor. Never in our entire history together have I known you to leave personal belongings of any description in the foyer, much less on the floor. So another thing was wrong with this picture, proving once again, children, that neatness counts. I crept like a mouse, sneaked into Ryland's room for the bat, arrived up here just in time to catch Brad sucking air. What the hell did you do to him?"

She mimed her blow, told him not to look at her like that. "It's the only punch they ever show you in those women's self-defense courses. You rushed him? What about the gun?"

"Never saw it until after I bonked him. I'm not like you. I don't go attacking guys with guns. And don't tell me you spotted the fake. No way does that thing look fake."

She explained.

"Good lord," he kept saying, "good lord." Then: "Suppose you still believed it was real. How were you going to dodge the bullets?"

"First, he hadn't used a gun to kill Rob, so maybe he wasn't much of a marksman. Mostly I was counting on the diary to throw him for a loop, soften him up for my punch. When he told me his sweet innocent violated hero was called Ashley, I knew I stood a real chance to rattle him. You're rattled, it throws off your aim. Come on, Dee. I couldn't just sit there and let him kill me. Which he was bound to do, once he'd exposed himself."

"You were going down the fire escape? What if he broke though the door and followed you? Cornered you down in the courtyard?"

"I wanted him to follow. The fourth step down from that window has been missing for months. I know it, and the kids know it, and someday real soon I'm going to call a welder and get it fixed. Meantime, can't you just imagine? Total darkness, his big clunky boot steps into pure space? Bumpety-bump-bump, down he goes, who knows how far and how many broken bones. It did occur to me that he might *not* follow, might run downstairs and out the front door, leaving me freezing and

190

clueless. And scared to yell, because at this point I still believed in the gun. Then I decided to ignore the contingencies, put my heart into what I knew that he didn't. The diary, the lavatory, the missing step. The step clinched it for me. I could *see* him, tumbling through space. Maybe he picked up on my confidence. Maybe that gave me an edge, let me make it to the lavatory. But you were the one who saved the day, Dee. What's wrong?"

A curious expression had crossed his face. "Tell you later. I think he's waking up."

"I'll call McGuire."

"Don't you want a private chat with young Brad?"

Until he asked, Olivia had wanted only deep hot water and three fingers of brandy. Extraordinary trait, curiosity. Give it an inch and it takes the whole bathtub. "Let me ask the questions, okay? I'll give you every sordid detail later, but a full replay with him listening and commenting . . . no. It'd finish me."

Together they hoisted Brad into Olivia's former hot seat, repositioned the overturned table and drafting lamp.

Dee complimented Brad on his moaning and groaning. "Marvelous range. From surly lout to plaintive lost boy, nothing's beyond you. Now then. You brought every bit of this on yourself, and Olivia has a few questions. You can talk through your headache or add a pair of smashed knees to your troubles. Your pick."

Grudgingly, with much prompting, he told them about the murder. Ever since Rob had thrown him out late Friday, he'd been in a sleepless torment over his lost bliss. By Wednesday night he couldn't take any more. He parked in the garage same as always, but walked to Mount Vernon as himself, not Kim. In an eerie reversal of Lori's practice, he saw Rob's lights on and hid in the bushes, hoping he'd come out. Soon after ten, he did. "Real light on his feet, whistling. I haven't slept for days, can't keep food in my stomach, and he's happy as a lark. So I . . . shut him up. Wouldja call the cops? My head's killing me, and I'm sick of the both of you."

Olivia ignored this. "So you weren't living there, on Mount Vernon?"

"Kidding? He kicked me out every night. Two, three in the morning, he didn't care. If he felt like it, he'd walk me back to the Commons garage. We'd see some mom and dad out on the town and he'd start feeling me up, stick his tongue down my throat. They'd be all tsk-tsk, except if you checked the dad you'd see, Oh, man, how do I get me one of them hot mamas in *my* life?"

"Where do you live?"

"J.P."

Jamaica Plain. "The neighbors there don't notice when a blond man turns into a dark-haired woman?"

"Duh. Rob made me keep the wig and all in my car, change in the garage. He said Kim was his creation, and he had exclusive rights. Okay with me. Beantown cops aren't exactly famous for enlightenment. They pull you over for a broken taillight, you better match the photo on your license. I don't have to tell *you* that."

Directed at Dee, this seemed a bid for gay solidarity. Very strange, Olivia thought, after his earlier fulminations and denials. But then, what about Brad wasn't strange?

Dee, looking progressively more and more baffled, had to break in. "But when you killed Rob, you weren't dressed as Kim."

"'Course not. Kim's a total wuss."

Dee glanced at Olivia, who gave him a go-ahead nod. "No witness could place Kim near Mount Vernon that night. Your neighbors couldn't connect you with the sketch in the paper. So why not burn the wig, disappear Kim forever?"

A wild gargle of protest. "You think this is about *sketches*? Saving my neck? I don't give a rat's *ass* about my neck. I don't give a rat's ass about anything! Rob's dead and she as good as killed him. *That's* what this is about."

"Lori killed him?" asked Dee.

"Jesus H. *Her.*" Brad stabbed a finger toward Olivia. "La Bitchola."

"Think of it as a parallel universe," said Olivia, heading for the phone. "I've had enough. I'm calling McGuire."

Dee moved to intercept. "Give me a few more minutes," he said in an undertone. "If we can hand the cops a written statement, it'll save a lot of noise and time."

About 9:45 P.M., Brad Lund forced his way into Olivia Chapman's house at what she believed to be gunpoint. Soon after, he threatened to kill her "faster than him," that is, Rob Mallory. Mrs. Chapman believed that her survival depended on encouraging Lund to air his many grievances against Mallory and, as it subsequently developed, against her. Mrs. Chapman, previous to this, had no idea Lund was harboring angry delusions about her. She had seen Lund twice, very briefly, in the company of Mallory. They had never exchanged any words; indeed, Mrs. Chapman had no inkling until tonight that Lund was anything but the woman Mallory had introduced as Kim Amundsen.

Lund drank several beers and smoked constantly. At one point his book of matches ignited; alarmed, he accidentally brushed the gun to the floor along with the matches. Mrs. Chapman then realized that the gun was fake but did not let on. Because Lund had used a knife on Mallory, she believed that he had a knife on his person. Urging Lund to continue his story, she waited for the right moment, and when it came she punched him as hard as she could, under the chin. She then ran to the lavatory, locked the door, and kicked out the window, intending to leave by the fire escape. Immediately following this action, Diego Quintero, a family friend who rents an apartment in the house, arrived on the scene. Arriving home a day earlier than expected, he had been alerted that something was amiss when he saw Mrs. Chapman's parka on the floor of the foyer. Lund, knife in hand, tried to stab Quintero, but Quintero overpowered him with a baseball bat.

"They're not happy with us," Olivia told Dee when McGuire and the rest of the police had left.

"'Course not. Recall your former client, the guy with the penthouse. Say his girlfriend, rank amateur, pulls off something makes your work look cheesy. How happy will you be?"

Olivia was too tired to explain that Val had hired her back. "Point taken. Also, I gathered from James that McGuire was tilting toward Lori. The money angle. I think James was tilting that way himself. Why not? Money's a wonderfully clear and comprehensible motive compared to what finally pulled Brad's strings. By the way, he claimed to be an equal-opportunity hustler. Didn't ring true, for some reason."

"I don't know what, if anything, he does with women. With men, my guess is the exchange of money gives him permission to have the kind of sex he can't allow himself otherwise. He's your basic fucked-up middle-class American guy, with a dash of artist–as–sex–outlaw. Some of his recklessness probably comes from being a prime candidate for AIDS, not that he'd have the wit to be tested. Are we through with the sordid details?"

Olivia didn't see any reason to tell him Brad had overheard in the Bentwood that she'd be alone in the house tonight. "I hope so," she said.

She was about to add that she was ready to call it a night,

when, abruptly grave, Dee launched into what had been left dangling by Brad's return to consciousness.

"It wasn't only the impossibility of James's being in two places at once that brought me running," he said. "Six, seven months ago, Rob started showing up at gay bars fairly regularly. He seemed to like talking to the drag queens, but I'd also heard rumors about him beating up people. Which is why I wasn't surprised to hear he'd been beating up his wife, remember? Anyway, I kept out of his way. Presumed straights who fool around on the great gay frontier aren't my dish of tea. When I heard about his girlfriend, I considered the drag possibility. But I didn't tell friend McGuire to round up the city's more demure queens and cross-dressers. What I did was put the whole business out of mind. When that sketch came out in the paper, I hardly glanced at it. Couldn't stand to make a connection to someone I knew, however slightly. Gay *omertà*. And it almost got you killed."

"I won't hear this, Dee. This has nothing to do with anything."

"Of course it does. Brad overheard me talking about visiting Mom last night. In the Bentwood."

"So he said."

"You knew? Why aren't you furious with me?"

She'd never tell him how betrayed she'd felt, back there on the stairs a million years ago. "For talking to your friends in public?"

This common sense got a dismissive wave. "Brad wasn't known to be into drag, and I never saw him with Rob. Doesn't matter. Others may have seen them together; I could have asked around. And if I'd looked more carefully, the sketch might've triggered something. Brad's been in my face a few times, trying to get me to *critique* his pathetic writing. God, how I hate that, 'critique' as a verb."

He squeezed his eyes, his whole face, shut, let out a groan of despair. "Why am I clinging to *usage*?"

"Better than flogging yourself over something you couldn't possibly control. Brad came after me because he's wired wrong. One minute he's gay-bashing, the next he's bragging about great sex with Rob. Kim's a hot mama; Kim's a total wuss. Rob dumped him and pissed on his novel, so I have to die. Bad wiring. Period. Unless you want to build the case that he was Rob's victim. I don't, offhand, but I'm open to argument."

"Brad's not the issue here. I did a terrible thing. E. M. Forster said if he had to choose between his country and his friends, he hoped he'd have the guts to betray his country. You're my friend, and gay *omertà* is the law of my country. I made the wrong choice."

"Stop that. Did the forensic shrink who read the diary warn me about projection and delusional rage? No. Did McGuire or James think to have my house watched? No. And not out of carelessness, either. They simply live in the same universe as you and I. You have to be like Brad to comprehend the other one."

Olivia had never seen her old friend look so sad and worn. She stood, held out her hand to pull him to his feet. "Hot baths for both of us," she said. "Float the dirt right down the drain."

He didn't even finish his favorite old Ajax commercial, the bubble-bubble-lub bass line. That's how low he was.

She pulled her down comforter up around her ears and sighed with pleasure. Curse the eighties all you like, a decade that gave us Belgian flannel duvets and sheets can't be all bad.

It was after midnight. Since James hadn't called by now, she probably wouldn't hear from him until morning. He must have heard the news so late he'd been afraid of waking her.

James. He'd wakened her, in a manner of speaking, last night. Just before sleep, this earth-shattering thought: Should her preparation for seeing him Friday night include changing the sheets?

Yes, she'd decided at agonizing length. The condition of the sheets was a contemptible hurdle, if hurdles were in store. (Of course they were in store. Who was she kidding? Even in *marriage* there are hurdles. Tiny ones if the marriage is a good one, but still . . . Nature's a prankster. You marry to ensure yourself, among other things, reliable access to sex. And then spend your life building and having to dismantle hurdles.)

After tonight's muck and terror, her clean-sheets debate, along with the mixture of trepidation, desire, and randy curiosity that had inspired it, seemed an artifact of some distant, genteel past. In a league with pondering whether any lady worthy of the designation should risk a waltz, bob her hair.

Bad enough she and James would need to maneuver past whatever putrid gobbets of the diary clung to their psyches. Reading is vicarious. Terror is . . .

Terror is male.

She sat bolt upright. Didn't mean that. Couldn't. She liked men; trusted them, on the whole, more readily than women. Certainly she had trusted Philip and Dee more absolutely than any woman friend she'd ever had. A natural outcome, she'd always believed, of being raised with brothers instead of sisters, of mothering sons instead of daughters.

Was terror, for her, male? Was this why Lori had irritated and exasperated but never really frightened her? And why she'd resisted believing her capable of murder?

Not that women, in their own ways, aren't scary. And by no means are they exempt from the failed-monkey charge. Rob's mother's response to her son's need of a funeral would amply qualify—assuming Lori hadn't been lying when she let drop that revolting piece of information.

Reminded, Olivia switched on the bedside light, opened the drawer of her night table, took out a pack of letters bound by a rubber band. Quickly she found what she was looking for: a sweet, virtually unprecedented note from Ryland thanking her for understanding about *The Mikado*: Things are great here. Like Dad used to say, day after day on the crest of Joy. Remember that? I finally figured out what he meant. It's really a neat idea!

Lori must have read this. Olivia hoped she'd seen it lying around, that she hadn't rummaged in the drawer, read everything, taken notes for some future best-seller.

Never let a stranger in your house.

James, lover of peanut butter, singer of songs, sublime kisser, conscientious and sexy telephoner, was still a stranger. Especially to a woman who, thanks to this night, felt not only violated but *altered*—in ways she didn't yet understand. A woman who'd been made, disturbingly, a stranger to herself.

She wouldn't bother changing the sheets. Sheets, for a while, were irrelevant. What was needed here was not excitement, adventure, risk, but wholesome, humdrum normality. Going to Symphony and choral concerts, biking if the roads cleared, cross-country skiing if they didn't, ice-skating at that North End rink with the harbor view. Week upon week of ordinary, simple pleasures, that's what was needed here. Innocent merriment.

Tomorrow, instead of oysters for two at home, she'd request a movie and sushi, out. And if that went well, next week she'd give a dinner party. Along with James she'd invite Nanda and Drew, Kitty and Vahan, Michelle Greene and her husband.

And Dee? Yes, absolutely. The more she could be with Dee in ordinary circumstances, pursuing simple pleasures, the better. How else to defeat the corrosive allures of guilt, remorse, self-reproach? How else to get back what they'd had before?